DESIRE
AWAKENED

AARON'S KISS SERIES BOOK 13

KATHI S. BARTON

This is a work of fiction. Names, characters, places, and incidents are products of the author's imagination or are used fictitiously and are not to be construed as real. Any resemblance to actual events, locations, organizations, or person, living or dead, is entirely coincidental.

WCP

World Castle Publishing, LLC
Pensacola, Florida

Copyright © Kathi S. Barton 2013
ISBN: 9781939865564
First Edition World Castle Publishing, LLC June 16, 2013
http://www.worldcastlepublishing.com

Cover: Karen Fuller
Editor: Eric R. Johnston

CHAPTER 1

"Ah, now I see where our communication has broken down. You are under the misguided opinion that we should care what Billy's mom does. Sadly, I think Billy's mom is a cow and should keep her opinion to herself. However, I'm a grown woman and have made my own way for quite some time, as you are well aware. So, the answer is still no. You are not now, nor are you ever going, to go on a skiing trip with Billy, his *au pair,* and her boyfriend, and I'm fairly certain that your dad would agree. And before you impart that no doubt sarcastic, witty reply that is currently rumbling around that head of yours, I want you to reflect a moment on your pitifully sheltered social life and the plans you have for next week."

He looked at the woman with so much anger that Lizzy could feel it across the room. The woman simply stood there and grinned at the little boy.

"I don't care for you very much right now. And at least I have a social life, pitiful or not."

Lizzy burst out laughing and quickly turned it into a hard cough when the woman looked up at her sharply. The kid had balls, she'd give him that. And so did the woman, for that matter.

"I can appreciate that. I don't like me much either most days. So, do we order, or would you like to go home and sulk with me? I'm up for either one, really."

The little boy looked at her for a few more seconds, then turned and looked at the desserts in the long glass case. "We can order, but I'm getting chocolate. And I'm telling my dad it's your fault entirely. You've driven me to a need for it."

Again, she laughed, but this time the woman didn't look in her direction.

"Yes, I can see that I have. I'm sorry. Just so you know, for as much as I get on your nerves, I love you ten times that much."

"I don't think that's even possible, 'cause I'm pretty irritated at you."

"And that goes without saying. Order, I have to get you back to your dad, you scamp."

Lizzy stood next to the counter and watched the little boy look over all the selections. Sam winked at her when she came from behind the counter and sat with her. She nodded to the counter.

"They come in here once a week. I've never seen the dad, but the woman is his sister. Her name is Donna. His is Mathew. I'm not sure why you'd care, but I saw you enjoying their banter too. He's a trip."

Lizzy had a moment to wonder why Sam was telling her this when the woman walked to the counter. She was limping. Lizzy looked at Sam.

"No, not what you're thinking. She was hurt as a kid, and since there was no real income, she wasn't able to get the care she needed. I doubt she even notices it. He's a cutie, isn't he?"

He was. Lizzy thought him to be around ten or so. He had hair as dark as the woman had light and he had to have the greenest eyes she'd ever seen. One of her aunts had green eyes, but this little boy's were so intense they defied even the shine of emeralds. She looked at Sam when she sighed.

"What is it?"

Sam shook her head, and the woman and little boy walked out.

"Sam, tell me nothing happens to that little boy."

"He's a human. And you know how your dad feels about me getting involved with human problems any more. He gets all medieval and throws a fit. I swear there are times when he's more possessive than even my own mate, Tucker." Before Lizzy could point out that she didn't know the half of her dad's wrath, she stood up. "If you go out there, you'll have to see to the woman first. The boy will make it if you help him later, but the woman won't."

The sounds of cars screeching when she opened the door startled her. She looked back at Sam, and she nodded. Lizzy took off in the direction of the gathering crowd and wondered what had happened.

The little boy was under the car. His legs were both broken. She started for him. Then she saw the woman. She looked into the car and saw that there was no one in the seat. Lizzy got in, careful of the glass and blood. The woman was half in, half out of the windshield of the car that the little boy was under.

"Get Mathew. I'm fine. Get my nephew." Lizzy could see that she was anything but fine and reached out to touch her. "Please, Mathew first. He's hurt."

"He's going to be fine. I have to help you or you'll die." The woman shook her head, and blood poured from her throat. "You're going to die if you don't listen to me."

Lizzy did the only thing she could do and bit into her wrist. Blood poured from the wound, and she knew that she'd bitten deep because she had never done it before. Lifting her wrist to the woman's mouth, she commanded her to drink, glad for the magic from both her parents. As the woman sipped from her wrist, Lizzy reached for her Aunt Sam.

"Call an ambulance. Tell them that the little boy has been…never mind, you know more than I do. I'm saving the woman, but I don't know. She's lost a great deal of blood. Her throat's been cut. I think whatever she's taking from me is going right back out."

"Cut into your other wrist gently and rub your blood over her throat. It'll heal the wounds quicker, but your blood will give her the boost she'll need to live."

She did as Sam said and watched the wounds at the woman's neck start to close off. Reaching into her mind, Lizzy gave her the will to live by telling her that her nephew would never forgive her if she gave up and died.

People started to gather around them, and Lizzy pulled shadows around them so she could feed the woman. When she stirred, Lizzy pulled her wrist away and sealed the wound closed as she'd done on the other arm. Stumbling out of the car, she moved to the little boy. Someone had pulled him out from under the car and she looked at his mangled legs.

He was crying in pain but wasn't screaming, she was sure. When she leaned over him, he looked at her. She wasn't sure if he was really seeing her, because he was in so much pain, but he spoke.

"My Aunt Donna. You have to help her. Please, that man tried to kill her." She looked at the car and noticed there were no plates on it, and then she remembered there had been no one in the car. "She can't die. Daddy will be so upset with her."

"Your dad might be upset with you if you were to die as well, don't you think?" He nodded and moaned. "Your aunt is going to be fine. So are you as soon as the ambulance gets here. You should try to sleep, don't you think?"

"I hurt. I'm trying to be brave like Daddy says I should, but I really hurt." She put her hand on his left leg, the worst, and pushed some of her power into him. "Don't tell him I was crying. Please."

"Never. And sometimes I cry when I'm happy. My daddy never makes fun or teases me."

When his leg was broken in one place rather than the entire leg crushed, she put her hand on the other and healed it completely, thinking how hard it would be for him to get around. She was weak with loss of power and blood. Knowing that she would have to sleep to rejuvenate, she moved away to leave them both to the authorities who had just arrived. She saw her Aunt Mel standing in the crowd.

"They were going to die."

Mel nodded, and that's when she realized she was just a shadow of herself and not really there.

"I'm not leaving him. He may need more from me and I can't leave him."

"Of course you can't. But I can't help you either with all these humans around. Do you think you can find someone to feed from? You need your strength or your father will come."

Her dad. He'd be really pissed with her for doing this. One of the rules of being a vampire was they couldn't change the outcome of someone's life without just cause. She looked at Mel and then around the crowds of people as the ambulance came to a screeching halt in front of her. She stood up when one of the medics asked her to move.

"No. Please. I want to hold her hand. Can I please?" They both looked at Mathew. "Please. She helped me."

The medic moved enough that Lizzy could sit next to him and take his hand. He was bloodied here as well, but not nearly as bad as his legs. As they put in an IV, the medic told her and Mathew what he was doing. Soon the little boy was drifting in and out.

"He's lucky. This could have been a great deal worse." She nodded. "I mean, it looks like he was run over, but the wounds aren't showing that it was as bad as it could have been. He might have lost both legs."

Lizzy watched the other people that had come in the ambulance help Donna. She was screaming now; her arm was lodged in the glass and they had inadvertently cut her deeper. Before Lizzy could think, she stood up and only stopped when Mel appeared in front of her.

"She'll live, Lizzy, but not if you murder the men hurting her. Take a deep breath and go back to Mathew. The blood running through her veins will help her now that you've given her a fighting chance." Lizzy looked at Mel before she nodded. "Go on. I've contacted your dad, and he and your mom will meet you at the hospital. Don't tell your father that Sam was involved. He's very protective of her right now."

Sam was going to have another child. This would give her and Tucker three, and everyone was so happy for them. Lizzy said she'd make sure he never knew and stepped back to Mathew as they were putting him in one of the three ambulances. She looked back at the car before getting in, memorized the VIN, and nodded. She would have to see what she could find from Pete.

~~~

Logan Burris looked up when the door opened. He stood when he saw the look on his secretary, Anna Pierce's, face. Something had happened. He came around his desk and picked up his jacket as she spoke.

"They're both going to be fine. They're at Good Sam and both will be in surgery by the time you get to them. I have a car out front and the police have agreed to escort you. Donna and Mathew were hit by a car."

He stilled, his body frozen from the inside out.

"Logan, you have to let go of my hand."

6

He released the grip he had on her hand and reached for the wall; the room was spinning. When he felt his head being shoved between his knees, he realized that he was about to pass out. When he started to stand, Anna held him down.

"Even if you're fine, I'm not. You scared the crap out of me." He put his hand on hers at his head and sat up slowly. "I've spoke to the doctor, Logan. I swear to you they are both going to live."

"Where did it happen at?"

She told him she didn't know and followed him to the elevator.

"I don't know when I'll be back."

"You just take care of the two of them, and I'll take care of what I can here. Call me when you hear anything or if you need anything. You have my number." He nodded, and the doors closed. He was nearly to the ground floor when he remembered he had three meetings set up for today and then dismissed it from his mind. Anna would take care of everything.

The police cruiser was stationed in front of his limo, and as soon as he was inside, they were off. Logan tried to tell himself that they would be fine, that Anna would never lie to him, but he couldn't help but think about his son and sister hurt. As soon as the car came to a halt in front of the doors of the hospital, he stepped out and rushed inside the area.

"I need to see my son and sister. Mathew and Donna Burris. I understand they are in surgery." The nurse nodded and reached for her phone. He watched her with a lot less patience than he normally had while she asked someone to come up front please.

"Doctor Reilly was in the building and he was taking over their care until you arrived to tell us who their doctor was. Your wife is a little upset and couldn't remember. She's up there now." A man came through the doors, and she nodded at him. "He'll take you up. Oh, and your wife has all your paperwork."

Logan was in the elevator when he thought about his wife. He wondered what the fuck she was doing here much less telling anyone she was his wife still. As soon as the doors opened, he was going to rip her apart. He just knew that whatever happened to his son had something to do with her. Either that or she would try and find a way to profit from it. He looked toward the desk when a woman stood up and started toward the desk as well.

She was covered in blood. Her suit coat that had once been a creamy white was now pinked in large blotches. Her skirt had a small handprint on it, and he knew at that moment that it was his son's. He arrived at the desk just as she did and looked at the nurse.

"I was wondering if you could find me some scrubs to put on, please? I don't want my father to see this on me. He's going to be mad enough as it is." The nurse nodded and stood up. "Thank you."

She started away when the nurse called her back. "Mrs. Burris, emergency just called. Your husband is on his way up."

The woman paled. Logan thought she was already very pale, but her creamy skin seemed almost transparent when she looked at him. He nodded to her, and she backed up two steps.

"I don't think so, honey. Come on and we'll find a place to have a talk about our son." He took her arm and pulled her down the hall. He was pissed off, but he wasn't going to embarrass them both by calling her out.

"I didn't tell them I was your wife. They just assumed it and I didn't want—"

"Let me guess, you heard the name Burris and decided to see if your pretend husband was the one in the paper. Good call on your part with that one, but I'm not going to pay you a fucking red cent." He shoved her in a chair that was in the

8

smallish waiting room only to have her come up quickly. "Sit down before I knock you down."

~~~

Logan opened his eyes and looked at the man standing over him, smiling. He tried to sit up. Was he really lying down? The man sat down next to him with a strong hand on his shoulder.

"She's still pissed at you. If you're a smart man, you'll wait here until she has a minute to calm down." He nodded toward the woman as he continued. "I've been knocked on my ass by her sucker punching me before. She held back with you."

"She hit me?" The man nodded and grinned bigger. Then he remembered what they'd been talking about when she'd hit him just punched him right in the face. He brushed the man's hand off and walked toward the woman as he worked his jaw. She'd hit him hard enough that he knew he was going to be bruised in the morning. He could have sworn the man said, "It's your funeral," but wasn't sure. She was talking to a woman who looked to be ready to deliver. He noticed there were a lot more people in the room than there had been before she hit him.

"I would like a word with you. Now, if you're finished socializing."

The pregnant woman giggled and walked to the man still sitting on the couch where he'd been. He looked back at the woman who looked even paler than before.

"If you tell me to sit again like I'm a fucking dog, I will show you that I can be one in a heartbeat. I will not be treated like that." He snorted, and she glared. Christ, all he could think about was how absolutely beautiful she was.

"What did you have to do with the accident? If you think to blackmail some sort of payment out of me, you're going to be sadly disappointed."

She looked at him, then threw back her head and laughed.

"If you don't believe me, we'll see when I have my attorneys contact you."

"I don't want, nor do I need, your money, Mr. Burris." She looked over his shoulder and groaned. When she reached for the wall beside her, he put his hand out to catch her. She looked ready to fall over.

The arm around his throat had him put both of his hands up in surrender. As the grip tightened, Logan felt his air shut off, and was just reaching for the arm when the girl spoke.

"Don't hurt him, Daddy. Please? His little boy and sister are the ones I helped."

He was suddenly free of the arm around his throat, but not the man himself. When he was turned around, Logan knew the true meaning of fucking pissed. This man seemed to vibrate from it. And Logan wasn't sure, but his eyes seemed to have changed to a deep red.

A woman, a very beautiful woman, stepped between them, and the man took a step back. When she tapped her foot, he took two more back. She turned to him and smiled.

"You'll have to forgive my husband. He's a tad possessive of his only daughter. I keep trying to tell him she's fine on her own, but he just insists that she won't be able to fend for herself." She took his chin in her hand and tilted his head to look at his jaw. "She did this to you?"

Logan nodded. "I'm sure I fell when she shoved me, but I can't be sure. I think I might have hit my head as well."

"Of course you did. No mere female would be able to knock a big man like you over." He wasn't sure, but thought that statement was a trap and said nothing. "Good boy. I'm Sara MacManus. The man standing over there with our son and his wife is Aaron. My son is Mac and his wife is Andi."

"I'm Logan Burris. My son and sister were in an accident. I came as soon as I could, only to find out that who I thought was my ex-wife, Lula Burris, was here claiming to be my wife.

Then I find her here." He glanced back at the woman who was sitting on a couch with her head leaned back and her eyes closed. "Is she all right?"

"She will be."

The doctor came around the corner, and they all stood up. Before he could say anything, the doctor hugged them all including him. "You're a very lucky young man that she was there when the accident occurred. Had she not been, the woman would be dead and the little boy would have lost both legs. As it is, they'll both be fine in a few days."

Chapter 2

Lizzy was feeling sick. She had listened to Thomas and felt so much better. The nurse gave her a pair of scrubs to put on, but thought she'd just go home and get to bed instead. Knowing that Mathew and his aunt were going to be okay, she started down the hall toward the elevators. Mr. Burris came up beside her just as she pushed the button.

"What did you do for them?"

She looked at him, not sure what he meant.

"To help them? The doctor said you had helped them. I just wondered what."

"Nothing much. I talked to them. And before you ask, no, I didn't take their valuables. I have enough of my own." He had the good grace to blush. She looked away. There was something very appealing about him.

"I was wrong to snap at you like I did. I thought you were someone else. My ex-wife has a tendency to leap right into the mess of things if she believes it will benefit her. I thought when they told me my wife was here, it was her."

Lizzy nodded.

"I'd like to tell you I'm sorry."

"Fine." She pushed the button again, trying not to think about how close he was to her. "I have to leave now. It was not so nice to meet you."

When the doors finally opened, she stepped in. Before they could close, he did as well. She was ready to blast him by telling him to get the fuck away from her when the shaft moved and she felt her head spin. Before she hit the floor, he pulled her to him.

The elevator took a sudden jerk and then stilled. She tried to get away from him, but he held her tightly. His soft words had her putting her hands on his shoulders to look at him in the dark. They were trapped in the elevator together.

"It'll be fine. You don't have to be scared." She told him she wasn't and he laughed. "Okay, I don't have to be scared if you hold me. I'm seriously freaked out here, and I'd hate to sob like a little boy."

Lizzy felt another wave of dizziness sweep over her and leaned her head into his throat. His vein was right there, warm blood flowing through it, and all she could think about was tasting him. Her tongue licked along the path of the blood from his pulse to just behind his ear and he moaned.

She felt the wall behind her press into her back as he lifted her up. Every part of her body was screaming at her to bite him and drink from him, but her mind was telling her no, to wait. When he kissed her, his mouth taking hers hard and with hunger, Lizzy felt her fangs drop in need. He groaned when she pulled back from him.

"We can't do this. You've no idea what I want to do to you right now." He buried his mouth at her neck and nipped. Jerking his head up, she knew she was lost. "I'm so sorry."

She bit his throat as gently as she could, and his hot blood filled her. His hands slid up under her skirt and she felt him slide his fingers deep into her. Reaching between them, she cupped his cock. Christ, she wanted him right fucking now. She lifted her head to tell him. But he pulled away and she nearly tumbled over.

He tore at his pants, and she watched as he freed his cock. When she reached for him, wrapped her hands around him, he groaned. Before she could taste him, he picked her up by her ass again and took them to the floor.

"I need to be in you." She nodded as he pulled her skirt up over her hips. "Christ, I've never wanted a woman this badly before."

He tore her panties from her and moved to her entrance. When he hesitated, she pulled him down to her mouth and kissed him. As soon as he slammed into her, she pressed her mouth over his open wound and suckled.

Pain seared through her, and she cried out against his throat. When he started to lift off her, she wrapped her legs around him and felt his cock jerk inside of her. He moved slowly now, the pain was now being replaced by the most incredible pleasure. She knew what was building, knew that her own release was close, and she sealed the wound at his throat with her tongue and moaned when he pinched her nipple through her bra and blouse.

"Come for me. I want...no, Christ, I need for you to come." He tore the buttons open and shifted her bra down over her breast as he sank his teeth onto her nipple. Even as he fucked her, he reached down and tilted her ass upward and she came apart.

Crying out, he lifted his head. His command for her to come again brought her, and his body stiffened above her as he joined her. She pulled him down and sank her fangs into his pounding pulse as he filled her. She felt his second climax even as his first finished. Lifting her head from his throat, she opened her vein at her wrist and offered it to him, wondering as she did what she was doing. Then his mouth took her, and she cried out again, a climax that rolled over her like a warm summer storm. As soon as he lifted his head from her wrist, she knew what they'd done.

"Christ, you're my mate." Thinking quickly, she took the memory of giving him her blood from his mind.

~~~

Logan pulled at his clothes as he watched her reflection in the mirror surrounding them. What the fuck had he just done? She was mumbling something, but he wasn't able to understand her. He was pretty sure he didn't want to know what she was saying. She was pissed, there was no doubt about that, but he didn't have any idea what she had to be upset about. Then he remembered something.

"You're a virgin." She laughed a bitter sound that for some reason tore at his heart. "You *were* a virgin. What the hell were you thinking that you made me take you in an elevator?"

She turned from fixing her blouse to look at him. He had a feeling that if he made any more comments right now, she'd murder him without thinking. Without taking his eyes from her, he leaned over and picked up her panties that seemed to glow under the emergency lighting. They were the brightest white scrap of silk and lace he'd ever seen. She snatched them from him and put them in her pocket.

"If you'll remember correctly, Mr. Burris, you were the one that grabbed me. I in no way started this." She leaned back against the elevator wall and glared at him. "You stay over there and I'll keep over here. That way you won't have to worry about me touching you again."

He wanted her to touch him almost as badly as he wanted to touch her. On the floor, against the wall, he wanted her. Badly. He wanted her to bite him like she had, sink her teeth into—

"Did you bite me?"

"I don't know what you're talking about. Why would I want to bite you?"

He had a feeling she wanted to do it again, but didn't know where that thought had come from when she shifted on her feet and pressed herself harder into the wall.

He took a step toward her, then a second, when the lights around them flickered. He waited to see if they moved or the elevator dropped them both to the lower levels and to their deaths. Logan watched her as the lights came on then off.

"What happened here? What did you mean when you said I was your mate?" The need to touch her was overwhelming and he had to put his hands in his pocket to stop himself from doing just that.

"We had sex. Nothing more. Would you please move back over to the other side? You're making me nervous." He took a step toward her, halving the distance between them. "Please?"

He felt her hunger. Not for food, but for him. Logan groaned and reached for her just as the elevator shook beneath them. Before he could pull her into his arms and hold her to his body, they started moving again. The elevator was fixed. He leaned back against the wall where she'd asked him to go.

"We had unprotected sex. And you were a virgin. That isn't just sex and nothing more, and you know it." He waited for her to say something, but when she didn't by the time the doors opened, he stepped in front of her, blocking the exit. "You'll tell me if there's a child. I don't know what happened in here, but I won't let you have a child of mine without you telling me." She didn't even look at him. "Are you listening to me?"

"Yes. But there won't be a child. I'm not ovulating."

He flushed at her bluntness and moved out of her way so she could move out. He felt a powerful urge to bring her back into the elevator and take her again. She turned to him before he could make a fool of himself.

"Your son said you'd be upset with him if he let his aunt die. What kind of person puts that responsibility on a child?" He didn't get a chance to answer, even if he knew how. "He never cried. Not once did he scream out in pain when I was with him. He was more concerned with his aunt dying and you being upset."

She turned and walked away from him. As the doors closed the sight of her from his view, he rubbed his heart. Something had happened here. He looked around and found her purse on the floor. Pressing the button to go back up to his son, he slipped it into his pocket. He told himself he'd give it to her parents but knew that he wouldn't. There was something about this woman that made him irrational, and he didn't like it.

As soon as the doors opened, a beautiful woman was standing there with a smile. He wasn't sure what she wanted, but she looked ready to burst with news. He started to step around her when she put her hand on his chest. Logan stood very still.

"You've no idea what happened, do you?"

He glanced back at the elevator floor, then back at her.

"She didn't tell you anything, and now you need to know all there is to know about her."

"I don't even know her name." He flushed when he realized what he'd said, but she only nodded. "Are you going to tell me?"

"No. And the purse you have of hers isn't going to help either. You'll have to figure that out on your own. But you have clues if you use them. Her father is going to be pissed at you when he smells you." She turned to walk away, and he stood there for several seconds until she turned back. "If you come on now and try not to piss me off, I'll protect you as best I can, but Aaron can be very possessive when it comes to the women in his life."

He walked up with her and watched as they all stood up when the woman entered. Then he remembered the last name. MacManus. As if the woman had heard him, she turned and nodded at him. Aaron came forward then. But the closer he got, the more...well, pissed he looked. When he was within touching distance, the woman put her hand on his chest.

"She won't survive if you kill him."

MacManus seemed to stretch, grow wider and stronger before his eyes. Then he shook himself and turned to his wife.

"Where is she? My sister, where is she?" Mac, Logan remembered his name being, stepped forward with a grin. "She didn't kill you, and I know you can't kill her, so where did she go?"

"I don't know. I don't even know what the hell is going on around here." Logan watched Sara as she moved, glided, toward him. "She looks like you a great deal. It's hard to believe that you have a daughter her age. I haven't known her that long, but I'm willing to bet she gets her temperament from her father."

Sara laughed. "And you'd be right. And thank you very much. She's gone home to rest. Are you coming over when you've spoken to your family?"

Come over? He didn't think so. "I'm sorry, I don't know what she's told you, but I've never met your daughter before today. And I'll be staying here until my son and sister go home."

Sara nodded and moved past him. She was down the hall when Mac and his wife passed him with a nod. Aaron moved up to stand in front of him, and the other woman simply stood nearby.

"Did you hurt her?" Logan shook his head. "Good. Mate or not, I won't allow you to hurt her."

"She said that. After we...when...Christ." He rubbed his hand over his face. "What does it mean? Mate? I understand the word, but she said it like it was a disease or something."

"No, not a disease, but something akin to a bond for life. She'll need you before your family is ready to leave. Will you help her?"

"She saved my family, according to the doctor. If she needs anything, money or whatever, just have her call my office." Logan reached into his jacket, pulled out his wallet, and handed him a business card. "If she needs to speak to me about...anything, have her call my office and I'll call her back."

Aaron handed him back the card. "It's doubtful she'd use this unless she used it to slit your throat. Good luck, Mr. Burris, I believe you're going to need it."

As he walked away, Logan tried to rein in his temper. Of all the rude men he'd done business with, this man had to take the cake. Aaron turned around just as the man reached his family. Logan was just pissed enough to poke the bear.

"She and I had sex today. I haven't a clue what her name is, and I'm sure you won't give it to me. But if there's a child, I have the right to know about it." Aaron bowed and stepped into the yawning mouth of the elevator. "Bastard."

After finding out when he could see his son and sister, Logan sat on one of the couches that the MacManus family had occupied. He pulled out his cell phone and called Anna. After telling her all he knew, he asked her to look someone up.

"Her last name is MacManus and her dad's name is Aaron, mother Sara. I'm not sure of the spelling of her name." He heard the catch in her breath. "You know something, tell me."

"Aaron MacManus and his wife Sara are reputed to be worth billions. They donate more money a year than you make in two. Sorry, boss, but if you know the MacManuses then I'm going to ask you for a job reference." She laughed. "Not really, but I've read that their son, Aaron as well, but goes by Mac, was recently married and is expecting their first child. There's another son...Daniel is his name, and I believe he spends a great deal of his time out of the country, as there isn't much on him. But the daughter? Let me see if I can find her name."

He waited for what seemed forever, but knew it had been only a few minutes. He knew before she came back that it wasn't going to be there. He thought of the purse, a wallet really, and took it out of his pocket. Money and a set of car keys, but nothing else. There had to be close to three grand in her wallet, and for some reason, it pissed him off that she'd put herself at risk by carrying that much cash.

"Funny, but there's nothing here mentioning her name. The article does say they have one, but there's no mention of her name."

He asked her to see if she could find it and an address for her.

"Sure thing, boss. But you should be careful with her. I may not remember her name, but I do remember reading a few articles about her that says she's pretty tough. Might even be as mean as you can be when a deal doesn't go your way."

He hung up and put the girl's wallet into his pocket again. Logan reached up and ran his fingers over his throat and shivered. He was sure she'd bitten him, and he didn't know why, but he felt a deep connection to her that made him ache to be with her again. He took the purse out again and sniffed it. He could smell her on it and held it in his hand while he tried to reason with himself what he was doing acting like a love-sick boy. When the nurse came out and told him he could see Mathew, he stood only to have to reach for the wall.

"You all right, sir?" He nodded. "You should drink something. Juice and a lot of it. Would you like me to bring you some?"

He nodded and moved toward the room with her. Juice sounded good. Very good. His mouth was practically salivating for it, and he asked her if he could have it now. She nodded and walked away. He had a feeling she knew why he needed it more than he did. Logan sat next to the bed and held his son's hand. He wouldn't be able to see Donna until she was out of surgery for a little longer. Her injuries were a great deal more extensive.

Logan finished off the juice before the nurse left the room, and she set four more in front of him. She told him she'd be back in a few minutes with a sandwich and more juice. Fifteen minutes later, she returned with the extra juice and what smelled like a roast beef sandwich as he'd just tossed the empties into the trash. He drank the last of them slower, his thirst about quenched, and ate the roast beef sandwich in three bites.

They let him see Donna two hours later. She looked like she'd been run over several times with a car. The police had come and gone, and he had a better picture of what had happened. He held her hand for the entire ten minutes he was allowed in the room with her. He met Doctor Reilly on his way back to Mathew's room.

"I'll have her moved down to his room in the morning. They both did well, thankfully. The police have taken pictures of them both for the report. They said that whoever hit them had fled the scene." Logan nodded. "I do hope you can find the person responsible for this." Logan thanked him again and went to Mathew's room. He had his eyes open, but they looked glazed in pain. He kissed his hand and wiped at the tears. Things already looked better.

Chapter 3

Lizzy watched the fairies fly across the field without really seeing them. She'd been at the castle for three days and still wasn't ready to go home yet. Aunt Mel had been trying to speak to her, but Lizzy wasn't ready yet. Besides, she wasn't sure herself what had happened and why. She wanted to talk to Mac, but he was busy with his own mate. She looked up when a shadow crossed over her. Shamus, the king and her uncle.

"Sometimes when you least expect it, the best things pop up. Did you know that we had nearly five hundred new brownies born yesterday?"

She smiled.

"If you don't talk to Mellie soon, she's going to have a fit and come gunning for you."

"She can wait until I'm ready. I only came here because she said I'd be able to think. I can't think if she's going to be pissy to me."

Shamus nodded and sat with her for a long while before he spoke again. "The little boy went home yesterday. His aunt will need a little more care, but she should be well enough to travel in a few more days. He asks about you."

She looked at him, knowing who he meant and that it wasn't his dad.

"He believes that you were an angel sent to save him and his aunt."

"A wolf was in the car. I have to let Bradley know, but I know all of them and it wasn't one of his pack. Do you know who it was and why he hated the woman so much?" He shrugged. "Is that a, 'I know, but can't tell you,' or 'I don't know' gesture?"

"Neither and both." She growled at him. "You have to go and talk to your mate, Lizzy. He needs to know what you and he are to each other. And the longer you stay here, the stronger your thirst for him is going to be. It won't be safe for you to be with him if you wait much longer."

"I know. He is completely blameless in this. But he has to know that I did bite him. It'll be hard for him if someone that is against my dad finds out and uses him against him." Lizzy watched the fairies as they flew over the field of wild flowers. "Shamus, do you suppose if I never left here he'd be all right?"

"You know the answer to that, Lizzy, as well as I do." He grinned as he looked over her shoulder. "But I believe my mate has taken the decision out of your hands."

Lizzy turned and saw Mel coming toward her with someone. She stood up when she realized who it was. She was going to fucking kill her. If she could actually do it. Mel was an immortal and couldn't die, but Lizzy figured she could do a world of hurt to her. Tess appeared in front of her.

"Behave."

Lizzy stared up at the beautiful warrior fae as Tess continued.

"You should know by now that here I can feel your every emotion. Don't hurt Mel and I won't have to hurt you."

Mel and Logan stood before the three of them. Shamus moved to shake hands with Logan, and Tess told him hi. Great, meeting the family on their terms couldn't be a good thing.

"You two haven't actually met, right?"

Logan nodded at Tess's question but didn't take her eyes off her.

"This is Elizabeth MacManus. Everyone simply calls her Lizzy. I'm Tess, by the way."

Logan turned to look at Tess, and she fluttered her wings and hovered over the ground for several seconds before touching back down. Logan took a step back, then another, before he looked at her. "Am I dreaming? I've had a great many strange dreams in the past few days. I'm going to hope you say yes and tell me that this is just another version of where you tell me what the hell is going on." He looked at Mel and Shamus, then back at Tess, before looking at Lizzy. "This is the first time I've been told your name, though."

"It's not a dream. You're in the Kingdom of Molavonta, the magical realm of Queen Melody, Mistress of Light, Keeper of Magic. This is her mate, Shamus, Warrior Fae of the Brianal Guard, King of Magic." She watched him shake hands with the two of them. "And this pain in my ass is my Aunt Tessa. She is Lady Tessa May Knight, Master of Arms of the Brianal Guard, Warrior Fae, Leader to the troops of the Queen and King of the Warrior Fae, mate to Nathaniel Tremont, Master of Arms of—"

"He's got it, Lizzy. We're all impressed that you remembered your genealogy." Tess put her hand out to Logan. "Pleased to meet you. Nathaniel said to tell you if you need advice on living with a vamp, he'd be more than happy to give it to you."

Logan took her hand and sat down. Lizzy watched him for signs of hysteria, but he only sat there. Mel and Shamus walked away, and Tess moved off a few yards. She was always around when a newcomer came to this world, but she wouldn't disturb them.

"This is a dream." She shook her head. "It has to be, otherwise I'd be going off the deep end right now, and that's not happening. What the hell did she mean he had advice on living with a vamp? A vampire?"

"Mel has you in a sedated state right now. She doesn't want you hurt, and Tess will hurt you if you disturb the natural order of things. It also makes the fairies nervous when humans are here. I think she's hoping they won't notice and leave this field unattended."

He looked over the field and back at her. "Of course. The field is very important. And where is this field? Wait, don't tell me, the Kingdom of Malt Balls."

"Kingdom of Molavonta, and there is no reason for you to be nasty to me. I didn't want you here." He looked out over the field again. "Maybe now that you're here, I can have someone explain why they brought you here. Then I can arrange for you to go home."

"I'm seeing this shit, but I can't make my mind wrap around the fact there is a dragon in the field beyond us and there are tiny little pixies in that field. What are they doing anyway?" She looked but before she could answer, he leaned back in the chair and spoke. "I've hit my head, haven't I? I haven't been sleeping well, as I've said, and I've hit my head."

"No, you've not injured yourself, and those aren't pixies but flower fairies. They get sort of nasty when someone calls them by the wrong name." He glared at her. "Well, they do."

"You think I give a shit? I don't care what they are. I want you to explain to me what the fuck is going on, how I ended up here, wherever here is, and how the fuck do I get back home?"

Tess turned to them and laughed.

"Does she have wings?"

"Yes. I told you, she's a fae. They all have wings." She looked up into the sky and reached for a messenger mist to come to her aid. A bright pink one was in front of them in seconds.

"My lady?" Messengers didn't have any kind of form, but were literally a cloud of energy that only looked like mist. The brighter the color, the younger they were. This messenger was only about seventy years old and very bright green. Lizzy had made her when she'd been about ten.

"Find the queen for me and ask her to allow me to take Master Burris home. Tell her that I'm not caving." The mist nodded and left as Lizzy turned to Logan. "Come on. I'll take you back to the gate."

~~~

Logan followed her through the field. He tried very hard not to look around, knowing that he was going to see something he couldn't erase from his mind. As soon as the castle came into view, he stopped moving and frowned when Lizzy continued to walk. She'd come back or he'd begin to believe what he was seeing. Either way, he knew he was fucked.

When she came back toward him, he watched her move. Her body was covered in a pair of lounge pants that had seen better days, a t-shirt that looked like something his son would wear, and she had no shoes on. Her hair, a glorious shade of the palest yellow, almost white, hung to her hips and curled slightly at the end. When she stopped in front of him, he wanted to reach out and pull her body to his, but knew on some level if he did, she'd hurt him.

"We have to go this way for you to get home. I can try to erase your memory of this place, but as soon as you pass through the doors, it'll come right back. Not how to get here, but what it—"

Logan pulled her toward him and kissed her. Her mouth was wet and warm; her tongue tangled with his over and over until he felt as if he'd touched every part of her. Reaching down, he spread his fingers along her back and pulled her closer, her breasts pressed against his chest. When her hands moved up his shoulder to his hair, he shifted her until she was riding his thigh. Cupping her ass, he pulled her up and down his leg until she moaned. He tore his mouth away and put his forehead onto hers.

"I want you. I want to take you right here and right now. I can't seem to get enough of you. Touching, tasting." He stepped back, dropped to his knees before her, and pulled her to his mouth clothes and all. "You smell delicious. I need to eat you."

He yanked her pants down to her knees and buried his face into her soaking panties. They were green, as green as the grass around them. When she curled her hands into his hair again, Logan couldn't have stopped if someone put a gun to his head. Then he felt the sharp bite of a knife at his throat. He didn't move.

"You're in a fucking field with like seven thousand other beings around you watching. Do you think maybe you could find a more public place to have done this?"

Logan glanced up at Tess, who had a sword to his throat.

"Stand up."

"Tess, back away from him."

He glanced at Lizzy and nearly took a step back as well. She looked…Christ, he wasn't sure what she looked like at this moment, but all he could think of was wild.

"He was going to take you. Here." Tess tensed when a low growl came from Lizzy. "All right, Lizzy. I won't harm him. Look, I've let him go, and my blade is put into my scabbard."

As soon as he was released, Lizzy moved forward and punched the other woman in the face. Tess didn't budge. She didn't acknowledge the fist to her mouth at all except for the small pearl of blood on her lip, which she licked away.

"You should fucking know better."

Tess nodded, but didn't look the least bit repentant. When Lizzy drew back to no doubt hit the woman again, Logan stepped in front of her. "Wake me up or whatever it takes to get me back to my family. This is stupid." She stared at him as if she didn't know him, then nodded once. When she touched his forehead, there was a slight pain and then nothing.

28

When Logan opened his eyes, he was sitting in a chair at the hospital. He got up to check on Donna but sat back down. What a fucking surreal dream. Logan had to get some sleep. His body was aching, and he was having the strangest erotic dreams.

Logan looked at his watch. The doctor was supposed to come and see her this morning, and it was after noon. What the hell? Going out of her room, he found a nurse and asked her when the doctor was coming in.

"I'm sorry, Mr. Burris, but he was here at nine. You missed him."

Logan shook his head but then remembered the dream. The man couldn't have woken him?

"Would you like for him to give you a call? He said he would tell you whatever you needed to know if you were to come in. Honestly, I had no idea you'd come in or I would have called him sooner."

Logan nodded and went back to Donna's room, knowing that he'd been there all along. This time, she was awake, and he sat on the corner of her bed. Over the past several days since she'd been getting better, he tried to get out of her what had happened when she and Mathew had been hurt. All she remembered was that she and Mathew had come out of the bakery and that a there was a loud engine. She mentioned the woman, but couldn't describe her. Logan tried hard not to think of the amount of glass they'd taken from her head that night or the amount of stitches they'd had to use to put her back together. She looked hurt, bruised, and cut up, but nothing compared to what the doctor told him could have happened to either of them.

"Did you talk to the doctor?"

Donna nodded.

"When can I spring you from this place? Mathew misses you."

"Friday. Said I was fit, but he wants to make sure of no infections." Her throat had been cut as well, and Logan thought about what the doctor had said about that. A mere eighth of an inch and she'd be dead.

"Good, Mathew misses his favorite aunt, like I said, and I sort of miss you as well." She smiled and told him she missed him also. They sat and talked about mundane things. He talked mostly while she nodded. When she started to nod off again, he stood up. She said his name softly and he came back to her bed.

"Find the woman yet?"

He started to tell her yes he had, but he only shook his head.

"I think...she gave me her blood." Then she closed her eyes. Logan couldn't move. He was terrified of what she'd just told him.

He stood over his sister long after she went to sleep. The same thought had kept circling around his head. She'd given Donna her blood. He reached up and touched the small area right below his ear and felt his wound tingle as he thought of the woman he'd made love to in the elevator. Had it only been a few days ago? And today? Was today only a dream?

He left Donna's room and headed down to his car. He was nearly to it when his phone rang. It was the doctor. After a lengthy conversation of him telling Logan again how lucky they'd both been, he confirmed what Donna had said; she could go home in two days. Before he changed his mind, he pulled out the piece of paper that Anna had given him that morning and dialed the number.

"Hello. My name is Logan Burris. My son and sister were hurt a few days ago, and I was wondering if I may speak to Aaron MacManus. Please tell him it's important."

"I am sorry to tell you, sir, but Master has retired for the day. My mistress is about. Shall I find her for you?" Logan told him that that would be great. "Please hold for a moment. If I should disconnect when I put you onto the hold button, would you please call again? I have yet to learn this new system."

Before Logan could say yes or no, he was disconnected. He started to call back, but wondered what the fuck he was doing. He was pulling into his building's parking lot when his phone rang again. Answering it with him, simply saying his last name, he was surprised to hear a woman's voice, an angry woman's voice.

"He asked you to call back. You've upset Duncan, and when he's upset, the household is upset, Mr. Burris."

He was nodding when he realized what he was doing. "This is Mrs. MacManus, I presume?" She said yes, but told him to call her Sara. "I'd rather just keep this unfriendly, if you don't mind. I think I talked to your daughter today. Some woman who Lizzy claimed was the queen of something brought me to her."

"That would be Mel, my cousin. I'm assuming you didn't piss her off as much as you have me. If you had, you'd be in the dungeon right now and not speaking to me."

He had a moment to think this whole family was insane. "Whatever. Tell your family to back off, Mrs. MacManus. I don't know what you guys hope to gain by this little game you're playing, but I'm finished with it. The next time my son asks me about her, or my sister mentions blood, I'm going to tell her that they both dreamed her up. Understand?"

"Of course. You plan to lie to the two people in the world who might be your only connection to your happiness and that of Lizzy. When you said you thought you saw her, what exactly did you mean?"

What did he mean? He wasn't sure now and leaned against his car as he thought about it. He started speaking, but really wasn't sure what to believe now.

"There was a castle and this woman with wings and jewels in her ears and along a crown she had on. And a sword, she had a sword at my throat. There was a dragon too." He rubbed his head and stood up. "Keep away from me. I'm under a great deal of stress right now, and I don't need the extra problems that your family is giving me."

She was quiet for a long time, and he thought she'd hung up on him. Looking at the time as the seconds ticked by showed him that he was still connected. She spoke before he could end the call.

"You do know that you called here, do you not?" He didn't answer. "Lizzy will stay in Molavonta until she is starved because she can no longer get what she needs from others. Do you understand what I'm saying to you? Lizzy is just enough vampire that now that she's bonded with you, she'll not be able to feed from anyone else and she'll die."

He felt a surge of anger when he thought of the "others," but realized what the woman had said. Of course Lizzy was a vampire. And he was the king of the world. Without saying a word, he disconnected the call and went into his building. He had more important things to do than talk to an insane person. It was nearly ten that night before he left his office.

When he reached his car, a man leapt out in front of him. Before he could move, Logan was doubled over in pain from something hitting him in the gut. He tried to stand, but another man grabbed him from behind and held him as he was hit with a bat. He felt his rib break and the air rush from his body. They told him he was going to die, and so would his family if he didn't back off on the sale of the Lacer Building downtown.

Then, just as suddenly as it started, he was freed and fell to the ground. Dropping his head to lean against the ground because he was seeing things blur before him, he lay down and closed his eyes.

"Can you stand?"

He tried to, but couldn't. Then Lizzy was helping him up.

"Come on, I'll take you to your house. Where do you live?"

He told her and must have blacked out, because the next thing he knew, he was lying on his bed. He mumbled a thank you and suddenly had to get up. He felt the urge to throw up as she helped him to the bathroom.

"Yeah, that'll happen only the first time. After that, it'll be better." Logan looked up at her. "You know that those men were going to kill you, right? Do you know why?"

"None of your business. I'm fine now. I'd like it if you left." She laughed, and he glared at her as he tried to make his way back to his bed. "I'm serious. I'd very much like it if you stayed away from me and mine."

"I can't."

He started to tell her she'd fucking better when she touched his forehead and said "sleep." Then a black void crushed over him.

CHAPTER 4

Lizzy tried to sleep in the chair in his room, but couldn't get comfortable. It was a chair, not a bed, and she loved her own bed. She looked at the one the idiot she'd saved was sleeping in. She wanted to crawl in there with him. Instead, she got up and left the room.

There was a maid in the hall who was trying to stuff a vase into her purse. She dropped the vase on the floor in front of Lizzy as she walked out.

"I'm pretty sure that's not yours," Lizzy said. The maid looked at the room behind Lizzy, and she let her think what she wanted. Lizzy crossed her arms over her chest and reached out and touched the woman's mind. This wasn't the first thing the maid had stolen from Logan, only the least expensive item in a long list of things over the past several weeks she'd been working for him.

"He'll never know if you don't tell him." The maid reached into her pocket and pulled out a gun. "Or maybe it would be best if you were not around to tell him what you think you saw?"

Lizzy was tired and just wanted to go back to the castle. Not really. What she really wanted to do was to go into the bedroom again and see if sex in the bed was anything like in the elevator. She had a feeling it wouldn't be. It would be phenomenal. Instead, she reached deeper into the woman's mind and seized it.

Within ten minutes, Melissa, the maid, handed over the gun. Lizzy also learned the name of the pawn shop and a list of things she'd taken.

"You'll get your big butt home now and bring back everything you stole from this house. And you'll do it tonight. If their things aren't back here by the time the sun rises, I'm going to put you into a world of hurt. And you so don't want to fuck with me tonight." Melissa nodded and turned to leave.

Lizzy wanted a shower, but first she needed to dispose of the gun. She stepped in Logan's room and slipped it in the nightstand. Then she walked down the hall, found an open door, and peeked inside. Mathew was trying to get to his own bathroom. He wasn't getting very far when she knocked on the door.

"Go away, Melissa. I told you that I don't want or need you in here." He mumbled something about privacy and looked up when Lizzy cleared her throat. "You."

"Yes, me. Can I help, or do you need me to go out?"

He looked at the bathroom, then at her.

"I can just help you inside, and you can do the rest. I'd hate for you to fall and hurt yourself."

"Okay, but don't stand outside the bathroom door. I can't...I won't be able to do anything if you're standing there."

She nodded and tried to hide her smile.

"That doctor said I should only move when I need to. How's a man supposed to get to the bathroom without it being a need?"

She didn't answer, afraid she'd embarrass him. As soon as she got him to the counter, trying really hard not to simply pick him up and put him there, she went to the other side of the room and looked out the window. It was getting dark, so she turned to the bed and started to make it up. She'd pulled off the dirty sheets when he opened the door.

"If you tell me where the linens are, I'll set this up for you," Lizzy said. He looked pale, but unless he asked, she wasn't going to offer to help him again. "You can sit in a chair for a few minutes, can't you? I won't be but about five minutes."

He nodded and asked her to help him please. Which she did and said, "The linen closet for this room is in the bathroom. My favorite sheets are on the bottom. Can you get those?"

It took her ten minutes to make his bed. And then another twenty minutes to help him get on a clean pair of pajamas after a quick sponge bath and brushing his teeth three times. He lay in the bed nearly as white as the pillows when he smiled at her. "I've wanted to do that for a week," Mathew said. "Melissa said I'd catch my death. I wanted to tell her that I'd been there already, but I didn't need to smell like it." Lizzy laughed and pulled the sheet up to his chest. "I could use a pain pill now, if you don't mind. They're in the bathroom."

Actually, there'd been something else that Melissa had tried to steal tonight. Lucky for poor Mathew Lizzy'd found them in her things before Melissa left. Lizzy went into the bathroom and got him a cup of water and put his pills on the counter after taking one out.

She sat down when he asked her to. "I don't know where my dad is, do you?" Mathew said. "He was supposed to come home and we'd talk. I wanted to tell him about Melissa and her not helping me. He said he'd try to be home by seven, but then he called and said he was running late."

"He's in bed." He flushed, and she smiled at him. "I'm not sleeping with your dad, Mathew. I just helped him to bed. He'd been...he's been working really hard lately, as you said, and was too tired to drive home."

Mathew nodded, and his eyes started to drift closed. He opened them when she stood up. He looked panicky, so she sat back down.

"Don't leave us. I heard you tell Melissa to bring back our stuff, but what if she comes back with some of her big friends? I'm still too hurt to help Dad protect you." She nodded and told him she'd stay until his dad got up. "Thank you. I don't think I know your name."

"It's Lizzy. Lizzy MacManus."

He smiled and nodded. She waited until he fell asleep, then waited another twenty minutes before she left him. Leaving the door open again, knowing that she'd hear him if he woke, she went back to Logan's room.

It was well after midnight and she was exhausted. Putting him into a much deeper sleep, she took off her pants, but left on her shirt and crawled into his big bed. Christ, it was heavenly. She was going to be out of here before she woke him, and then she'd have someone come and watch out for the two men. She closed her eyes, wondering if Logan would notice a wolf in his house. She smiled and went to sleep.

~~~

Logan opened his eyes slowly. He hurt so badly he nearly cried in pain. Then he realized he wasn't in his bed alone. Looking to his right, he saw the outline of a body and reached out gently to touch it. When she moaned, Logan felt his cock come to life.

It was the fruitcake. What the fuck was she doing in his bed? Better yet, how the hell did she get in? Logan nearly groaned when she shifted on the bed, and did so when she slid her leg up his to his hip. He wasn't sure how his hand had moved so quickly to grab her and hold her there, but he was glad that it had. Logan looked at her face and saw that she was looking at him.

"You're supposed to be sleeping. I put you into a very deep sleep that you're not supposed to be able to wake from unless I allow it."

He moved her leg up higher on his hip and watched her face.

"You can't be serious. You have two broken ribs and a busted lip."

"I want you. Sit astride me and ride me. It won't hurt as bad." She started to pull away, but she was there now, and he wasn't going to let her go.

"You think I'm nuts, remember? You told me to stay away from you." Her voice had darkened and grew husky. "Logan, we can't do this. You don't believe in me."

"I believe you want me as much as I want you." He slid his hand down her thigh to her mound and felt her panties. "You're wet already. I've changed my mind. I want you astride me, but now I want you over my mouth. Come here, Lizzy."

When she shook her head, he wanted to demand that she do as he told her, but he wanted her too badly to piss her off again. When he slid his finger along the point where her thigh met her nether lips, she rolled into him. Moving her panties out of his way, he slid into her. Her moan made him ache.

"You're going to hurt yourself if you keep this up."

He didn't care, and the way she was riding his fingers, he was pretty sure she didn't either. He begged her to move over him again so he could taste her. This time, she sat up on her knees and looked down at him.

"Take off your shirt and bra. I want to see you this time." She unbuttoned her blouse and dropped it on the floor behind her. Next came the bra, a pretty strip of lace and silk that matched the color of her panties. She stood up and pulled them off as well. His cock ached to be inside of her. "Come here, Lizzy. Please, I want to drink from you again." He knew on some level that they shouldn't be doing this. That he should demand that she leave him, but like every time he was near her, all he could think about was taking her, fucking her, and touching her. But not necessarily in that order.

Instead of moving over him, she reached out to run her hand over his cock. Logan was naked except for his boxers.

"I want to feel you inside of me again. If I do as you ask, will you let me bite you again? I'm part vampire, Logan, and I need you to live. Will you let me?"

Hell, he wanted to tell her if he could come in her again, she could suck him dry for all he cared. Instead, he nodded and reached for her. The pain in his ribs prevented him from reaching for her breast when she was over him, but she seemed to understand and leaned over him, her left arm above her head and the other on his chest. Her nipple was right there for him to suckle.

As soon as he nipped at her, she moaned. Moving slowly, he ran his hand down her ribs, careful of his own, until he cupped her naked ass. She let him guide her over him.

Her pussy wrapped around him, and she arched her back up, bowing from his mouth. He pulled her closer to him, and she rode him, soaking his cock as she moved. When she sat up, Logan held his cock while she moved down over him. When he was buried to his root, she stilled.

"You feel good inside of me." She rolled her hips. "Hum, that's wonderful. I feel as if I can feel you to my throat."

Wrapping his hand over her hip, he showed her how to move. Soon she was riding him hard and fast, her face perfect in her pleasure. Watching her was amazing, and he wanted to see her face when she came. Reaching down, he pressed his thumb against her clit and she came.

She buried her hand over her mouth and screamed behind it. His balls tightened then, ready to empty into her, when she leaned over him and kissed him. Her tongue fought with his, dueled hard and quick jabs like he wanted to do to her body.

As she tightened around him again, his climax rolled and exploded from him. When she moved her mouth to his throat, he felt her bite. His release had him rolling over and pounding into her. She cried out against his flesh as she came again.

Logan felt the urge to bite her, the need to sink his teeth into her. When she lifted her head, he looked deep into her eyes and felt a connection snap into place like a rubber band against a wrist. When he looked down at her, he watched as she sliced a nail across her heart, and he dropped down and covered it with his mouth. He suckled hard on her blood, and his cock jerked to life again. He came hard after only two strokes, and when he did, he knew that whatever he thought about her, she wasn't leaving him. At least not until he had some answers. There was no way she could believe that she was a vampire. She liked to bite, sure, and he found he liked that, but that didn't make her a blood sucker.

The next time he woke, he was alone in bed. He touched the pillow next to him and it was cold. She'd been gone a very long time. Rolling to the side of the bed, Logan sat there with his head in his hands, and that's when he noticed his ribs. They weren't bruised. Not only that, but they didn't hurt. Standing up, he made his way to the bathroom and turned on the light. He was fucking healed.

He turned to his right, then left, and didn't see anything. Reaching in, he turned on the shower and noticed it was damp. Reaching for the towel on the warmer, he noticed the one hanging out of the hamper and pulled it out. It was damp too. She'd taken a shower.

Making short work of his own shower, he dressed in a pair of jeans and a t-shirt and made his way to his son's room. He nearly fell to his knees when he saw he wasn't there and that his bed had been made. He was tearing down the stairs when he realized that if someone had kidnapped him, they wouldn't take the time to make the flipping bed. He heard them before he saw them.

"You can too. Watch." Her voice and his son's laughter had him pausing outside the door to the kitchen. "See, look, you just have to hold the pan like this and give it a good shake."

He had to know and walked in to see his son flipping a pan of hash browns into the air and catching them. There were a few pieces that didn't make it, but the pride on his son's face was worth the mess. Lizzy looked at him as he stood there.

"Hi, Dad. Lizzy can cook like a pro. She was showing me how to work a griddle."

He nodded, but didn't stop looking at her.

"She and I are gonna have puffy pancakes. You want some too?"

"Sure, son, that'll be great."

She moved from the cook top to the sink, then back to the island again and wouldn't look at him anymore. He thought about reaching for her, but didn't know what to say once he got her there. He needed to see how deeply she believed she was a vampire, of all things. She looked at him, he saw the hurt in her eyes, and he had to turn away. Instead, he looked at the stuff on the table and picked up a watch he'd been looking for and thought he'd lost.

"Melissa brought it back. She stole it all. Lizzy told her to bring it back, and with the keys she'd made too. She sure had a lot of our stuff, huh, Dad?"

Logan glanced at Lizzy, who had her head buried in the refrigerator.

"She was stealing our stuff and wouldn't help me get a sponge bath either."

Sponge bath? Stealing? He helped Mathew to the chair and put his crutches against the wall near him. He walked to the island where Lizzy was and noticed that she was wearing the shirt she'd had on last night and her feet were bare. When she noticed him looking at her feet, she stepped behind the island and huffed at him.

"I didn't have time to put any shoes on when I left. And after we…"

She blushed, and he wanted to make her do it again. He moved toward her, forgetting that he wanted to talk to her and why. "After we what?" Her skin was warm and soft. "After we what, Lizzy? What did we do that has your face heating up?"

He moved back as the stove timer buzzed. Lizzy reached for the little timer, turned it off, and opened the door. The smells radiating from it made him groan. Nothing had ever come from that thing smelling that delicious. He moved when she took the large muffin tin from the oven and poured the contents out onto the counter.

He helped her put them in a bowl and then took them to the table. He hadn't noticed the first time, but there were jellies and jams on the table, as well as syrup and butter. He sat down when she told him to. She brought another plate to the table, and he watched his son talk to her.

"You should have seen her last night, Dad. She was so cool." She wouldn't look at him as Mathew continued. "She told Melissa to get her butt home and bring back your stuff before she put her into a world of hurt. I don't think she believed her at first, but then she took her gun."

Logan's fork was halfway to his mouth when his son said "gun." He dropped it when she stood up. When Lizzy tried to go around him, he grabbed her arm . "Sit down and finish your breakfast." He said it low, but was sure she'd heard him. When she sat and pushed her plate away, he pushed it back. Mathew looked at them both.

"I didn't mean to get you into trouble, Lizzy. But you were really brave for protecting us," Mathew said and played with the food he'd been enjoying so much before. "I should have kept my mouth shut."

"You're all right, kid," Lizzy told him before he could say anything. "He was gonna be mad at me when I gave it to him anyway. You just made it easier for me. Now eat. I have to get back to the…to where I was staying soon."

"You can't stay here?" Mathew asked in disbelief. Lizzy shook her head. "But you have to. Dad has to go to work, and Melissa isn't coming back. Who'll help me today?"

"I'm sure your dad will stay home. I can't stay, buddy. I can't…there are things going on you don't understand, and at my age, I don't always say what's proper when a kid is around." She ruffled his hair as she walked around to his side of the table.

"At your age," Logan said. She glanced at him when he realized he'd spoken out loud. "You can't be any more than twenty-three or twenty-four."

She didn't answer him, and he found that now he needed to know. Before she could go back to the sink again, he touched her arm and asked her how old she really was.

"Do you believe what you saw yesterday? What you were told?"

He glared at her and shook his head.

"Then what's the point? I won't waste my breath on telling you again what I am."

He helped Mathew up and to the bathroom as she cleared the table. When he came back, she was wiping it down. He jerked her around to face him when she tried to avoid him again.

"You believe you're a vampire. You want me to believe that yesterday I was in a queen's kingdom with fairies and dragons. You bit me and made me…I sucked your blood too. So does that make me a vampire also?" He pulled her to his body so she could feel what she did to him. "Does you thinking you're a vampire make you come harder?"

44

He watched her face harden. And when she drew back her hand, he let her hit him, almost welcoming the slap he knew she was going to give him. He knew the moment he'd said it he shouldn't have. And when she pulled away this time, he let her.

"You might believe this." She lifted her arms up and the room exploded in light. Covering his eyes, he fell back against the counter. When the light dimmed, he saw that the entire kitchen was spotless and, most importantly, she was gone.

CHAPTER 5

Sara watched Lizzy pace for a few minutes and then leave the room. Duncan stared after her, but said nothing. He was worried about her, as they all were. Sara felt she had to do something or Lizzy would go back to the castle again and not return this time.

"My lady, if you do not mind me saying so, Miss Lizzy is in need of something more than the toast that she is not eating. Someone must call her mate and make him understand," Duncan said.

Sara nodded.

"I would like to do so, if you do not mind. Miss Lizzy is my friend and I would like to see her happy again."

She nodded again. Duncan would more than likely confuse the young man, but then he might be curious enough to come to the house. Sara stood up and moved to the counter to get another glass of tea. "Do you know where his office is?" He said that he did. "You go and talk to him and see what you can do. If he has any question you can't answer, let me know."

"I will, my lady. I will show him the error of his ways and if that does not work, I shall have to resort to violence." He clenched his fist and pretended to fight. "I could make short order cook of him soon enough."

"I'm sure you could." She smiled at his newest missed meaning of a word. "It's make short work, Duncan, not short order cook." Sara went to her office and began answering emails from their subjects and was nearly finished when Duncan came in with a briefcase and his keys.

"I shall return posthaste, my lady. If you should require anything from me while I am out, please call. I do have my cell phone."

He was gone less than ten minutes when Lizzy came into her office. She sat down and stared at the window for a long time before she spoke. Sara knew that whatever she said, she wasn't going to like it.

"I'm going to Molavonta. I've talked to Tess, and she said I could hang around with her and Nathaniel for a few days, then I think I might..." She got up to pace, something she and her father did when they had a problem to solve. "I'm going to move there. I like it there well enough, and Mel said she'd leave me alone for the most part. Draco said he'd show me how to sword fight."

"Don't do this, Lizzy. He'll come around." She was already shaking her head. "Please try and talk to him again. Maybe after the other day, he'll be more open."

"He won't and we both know it. He refuses to see me for what I am. And now that I've drank from him, I won't be able to stay here without stalking him. I won't go rogue because the Fates have decided that my mate is an asshole."

Sara smiled, remembering her own asshole of a mate a long time ago. "You'll regret this. You can hide from him, but it won't lessen your need for him. And if you come back here, you'll hurt him when you do feed from him." Lizzy nodded and turned back to her. Tears were in her eyes, something she'd not see her daughter do for decades.

"He refuses to believe in me."

Sara wanted to find the man and kick his ass. She felt the stirring of her mate as he spoke to her.

"Not if I get to him first. Ask her to wait until tomorrow. I would like to speak to them both."

Sara told him she didn't think the man would come over.

Oh he'll be here. Trust me."

Sara smiled. "Your father would like for you to wait until the baby is born if you could. I'm sure that Mac and Andi would want you there as well." Aaron told her good thinking, and she continued begging Lizzy. "I would hate for him to not tell us the name of the baby because you're not here."

"I'll try." Lizzy left the room a few minutes later, and Sara leaned back in her chair. Her children were so stubborn and pigheaded, much like their father. She smiled when she felt him touch her mind.

"I'm not in any way the cause for their stubbornness. I believe that rests solely on your shoulders. Mac is mellower, like me," Aaron said.

Sara snorted.

"You don't believe me?"

"No, I don't." She smiled sadly. *"When the two of them finally figure this out, it's going to be explosive. You know that, don't you?"*

"Yes. And it'll be good for them both. Bradley said she came to him about the wolf in the car. The bat that she'd given him yesterday also had been used by a wolf. What do you think is going on there?"

"I don't know. But just so you know, Duncan is going to talk to Logan. It might confuse him enough that he has to come here to get a translation. He had a briefcase when he left."

"Heaven help the man then. I love Duncan dearly, but you know as well as I do that he can be a tad much. Especially when he gets angry. Then you can't understand a word he says."

Sara nodded. But Duncan loved Lizzy and always had. He would fuss at her more, but everyone, including Lizzy, knew that she was his favorite. Aaron told Sara he must rest, but wanted to know if later she'd come down and rest with him.

"You know as well as I do that there will be no resting. You want to have sex." She smiled when he agreed. *"What if I don't want to wait? What if I come down there right now and join you in that huge bed and we use every square inch of it?"*

"Come to me now, Sara. My cock aches to be freed and deep inside of you. Come to me and show me what you want."

She rushed to the lower levels, naked by time she got there.

~~~

"Logan, there's a man here to see you, he said his name is Duncan. He's from the MacManus household. He said it's important. And he also said that if you refused to see him to tell you it's about Lizzy." Logan looked up at Anna when she spoke and she nodded. "He's the cutest little man I've ever seen."

Logan sighed. Lizzy. He'd not slept well for nearly the week since she'd been gone. And whenever he did close his eyes, he thought of the fact that she believed herself to be a vampire, of all things, and the way she'd left him, but more about the way she responded to his every touch. "Tell him that I don't want to talk about Lizzy with him or anyone else—" Duncan moved past Anna and into his office. "See here, Duncan, I have work to do. You'll need to make an appointment."

Anna went out and closed the door behind her. He looked at Duncan. He was smiling as if he knew a big secret.

"I have asked my lady to help. She said to tell you that the young lady is not harmed, but believes that you have given me permission to come to speak with you." He sat down at his conference table. "Come see what I have brought you, Master Logan."

Logan looked at the files on his desk. He'd been looking at them every day and was still no closer to figuring them out than when Anna had handed them to him. He got up and walked to the table as Duncan opened his briefcase.

It was the oldest-looking case he'd ever see. Worn in places so badly that the leather was white. But it was well cared for, and he could see that the man who held it loved it. Logan would bet that someone important gave it to him and that Duncan treasured it as much as he did the friendship between them. Logan took the first picture that he handed him.

"The day Miss Lizzy and her brother were born. As you can see, they were beautiful babies. See the bruising around Master Mac's throat? He was nearly not born at all. Lady Pete delivered them by magic and spoke to the two of them before they were born. Miss Lizzy said that Mac could be born first, you see, so that he'd be able to be the oldest."

Logan handed the man the picture back. She was an adorable baby. Chubby cheeks and blue eyes. He took the next item. It was a birth certificate. It took him several seconds to realize what he was supposed to be looking at. Duncan nodded when he saw the date of her birth.

"According to this, she's nearly eighty years old. That's not possible. Why would you go to the trouble of doctoring this up when it's so obviously not true?"

Duncan nodded and assured him that it was. "You should look on the World Wide Web, Master Logan. Look up Lady Sara's name. There are many articles about her as a pilot as a younger woman. You'll see that she is nearly twenty-five years older than Miss Lizzy. And my master is over seventeen hundred years old. He is a true master of his realm."

Logan shoved away from the table.

"Everything I have told you is true. Here are more things if you wish to see them."

"Why are you here? Did she send you? Is she pregnant and she's too scared to tell me?" He found that there were times,

51

more often than not, that he wished she was. He wanted to see her huge with his child.

"No, she is not. But she is going away. She has spoken to her mother and has told her that she will live in Molavonta for the rest of her life. Miss Lizzy believes that you will not want her." Logan sat down at his desk as Duncan continued. "You have not asked after the men who tried to murder your son and sister. She is working on the case. She will crack it, I believe, as she is very good at solving things."

"My sister and son were victims of a hit-and-run. No one tried to murder anyone." He looked at Duncan when he handed him an envelope. He opened it, then read it and looked up at Duncan again.

"Master Bradley has a man looking into it. The bat had the scent of one of his kind, but not of his pack. Master Bradley is a kind and generous leader and will do what needs to be done to make this right."

Logan tried to shy away from the word pack and opened his mouth twice to ask Duncan what he thought the word meant. When Duncan handed him another piece of paper, it was an article dated nearly seventy years ago. It was about the young woman, Airic, and how she'd been found.

"You met her at the hospital. She and her mate, Master Bradley, live nearby the MacManus estate. They have several thousand members of their pack, all of them friends of your Miss Lizzy."

Logan looked over the things as he was handed them. He wasn't stupid, but he was beginning to think that there was more here than some doctored papers. There were birth records for others too, some he'd met at the hospital, others he had never seen before. But there were pictures of them; recent ones according to Duncan, and all of them were of people who were over a hundred years old.

Logan started to speak, but the room seemed to vibrate with something. Before he could stand up and throw Duncan to the floor to protect him from whatever it was, a beautiful woman was standing in front of him.

"Hello, Dunc, my man. Aaron sent me to retrieve Mr. Burris here." She winked at him. "My name is Zane. Would you like to do this the hard way or…well, my way is going to be hard too, but you can choose your pain level."

Logan tried to wrap his mind around the fact that she'd just appeared in the room. Before he could ask her about it, she stretched out her arm and pulled up her sleeve. There was the most beautiful tattoo of a knife he'd ever seen. She ran her finger down the length of it as he watched and when she got to the handle, she began pulling it from her skin until she was standing there with it in her hand.

"Mother fuck."

She smiled at him when she handed it toward him pommel first.

"I don't think so. I don't know what's going on here, but I'd like for you both to leave."

"Can't. Aaron, as much as I'd like to disobey him the rest of the time, said I was to bring you to him. And since he can't leave the house right now, he sent me." She looked to her right, and he did too as yet another being shimmered into the room. It was the king Shamus

"Get him out now. To the castle. They come for him."

Before anyone could move, Lizzy was there. She wrapped her arms around him and told him to close his eyes.

"Zane, the woman. Duncan, my arm."

They were instantly in the castle again. Logan moved to the sofa that seemed to move further away the closer he got to it. When he was sitting down, he looked up at Anna who was simply standing still.

"She can't see any of this." Logan looked at Zane as she continued. "As soon as it's safe, I'll have her taken home and she won't remember any of this or before. Her wounds have been tended to."

Someone came forward and handed Lizzy a bag, and he watched her as she opened it.

"If you'll lay back, I'll see how badly you were hurt." Lizzy sounded so strange to him.

"Hurt?" He looked down at his leg as she ripped his pants open. There was a long slice in his leg and he closed his eyes against it.

"It's wolf. I can't seal it without Mel's permission." Logan watched Lizzy as she cleaned the wound and tried to think what had happened. "They came for you. The wolf pack that wants you dead. They were attacking even as I came to you. I'm sorry you both were hurt. But I couldn't stick around long enough to get a good read on their minds, but it has something to do with a building."

"The Lacer building. That's what I'm trying to purchase along with five more in the downtown area. The gentlemen who came to the parking garage that night said that they were going to…Christ, Mathew and Donna."

She pushed him back in the chair. "They're safe. Bradley has been having pack watch your house for a couple of weeks now. Nothing will get past them."

Logan was overwhelmed again. So much so that he started thinking that everything she and the others were telling him was true. He lifted her chin up with his finger. "Show me."

Lizzy hesitated for a few seconds, then opened her mouth. Her fangs lengthened and sharpened. He could feel the place on his throat burn. "How much…what else? I know there's more, but…" He watched as she taped the gauze over his wound closed. "When you…give me your blood, you heal me?"

"Yes. Vampire blood is very powerful, but mine more so. My mother is the cousin to the queen of magic, as I've said before, and her blood runs through our veins like my dad's does." He lifted her chin again when she wouldn't look at him. "I'm going to make sure you're taken back now."

When she stood, so did he. She started to back away, and he pulled her back. He didn't pull her against his body as he wished, but he did hold her. When she looked away, he said her name softly.

"Look, Logan, you've made it perfectly clear what you think of me and what I am. I don't have the energy or the willpower to be nice to you right now, so if you'll go with Nathaniel, I can get back to what I was doing."

Without warning, a man appeared near them. He had to be similar to Tess—they were marked alike. But where she was bejeweled, he wore a single earring. He nodded to the man when he bowed. "I am Nathaniel."

Logan looked at him and said, "Walk with me. If I have to leave, I'd like to ask a few questions first."

Lizzy looked at Nathaniel.

"Not from him, but you. I'd like you to answer a few questions," Logan said.

"My lady?" said Nathaniel.

They both turned and Logan stepped in front of her. A troll, or what he thought was one, laughed.

"I would rather die than hurt her, but as she is your mate, I can understand. I have come to tell you that I've been instructed to bring the boy and woman here. They are in your chambers. There has been…an attack was made on the home of Lord Logan."

Logan stiffened and turned to her. "Where are they? Can you take me to them now like you brought me here?"

"My lady, I don't think that—"

Lizzy raised her hand and the troll said nothing more, but bowed again and stepped back. She wrapped her arms around him and told him to close his eyes again. A rush of air and he heard his son laughing.

"Dad, come look at this."

He pulled away from Lizzy, but before he could take more than half a step, she crumpled in his arms.

"Dad?"

"There might be someone in the hall; run and tell them to get a doctor. Quick, son." Logan took her to the big bed and laid her down. Then watched his sister as she walked across the room and helped him cover her up. He could only stare at her. She wasn't limping, nor was she bruised.

"That man, I don't remember his name, he said it was the magic of the castle." She looked down at Lizzy. "What happened to her?"

"She's dying," Mel announced as she walked into the room.

Chapter 6

Aaron watched the young man as he paced the room. Logan was completely out of his element, yet he wasn't acting like it. As the man paced by him again, it was all he could do not to reach out and hug him. He was taking the news much better than he would have.

"So if I do as you said and feed her, she'll be all right?"

Mel shook her head, and Logan stretched.

"You said she was dying and needed blood," Logan said. "If I can't give her that, what the fuck use is it for me to be her mate?"

"I'm going to pop you in the mouth if you don't calm the fuck down," Mel said, just as tense as the young man. "I said she is starving, but it's not just blood. Don't you fucking listen?"

"Mellie, perhaps if you—"

"I swear to Christ, Shamus, if you tell me to calm down again I'm going to stab you in the heart. I am as calm as I can be." Aaron snorted, and Mellie turned on him. "Your daughter is lying in one of my guest chamber—*dying* and you're making noises out of your nose like a hog. Say whatever you will or get out of my castle."

Aaron looked at Logan. "She's been here instead of home. The castle has magic surrounding it so that as a vampire, like

Lizzy is at the moment, even my blood won't heal her. She needs you."

"What do you mean a vampire like she is at the moment? Isn't she a vampire at your house too?" Aaron shook his head. "Then you'll have to explain that better than miss fancy pants there because I don't see the difference."

"She's not really a vampire at your house, is she, Mr. MacManus?" They all turned to Mathew as he continued. "She's a princess, huh? And she needs a knight in shining armor to wake her up."

Aaron knelt down before the boy. "That's right. And what does one have to do to wake a princess?"

"It's really a girl's story. I read it because it was extra credit at school. I wanted to read *Swiss Family Robinson* by Johann David Wyss, but it was taken by a seventh-grader. And he said he lost it." Mathew looked at his dad. "You have to love her. That's all. The kiss won't work unless you do."

"I have that book in my library at home, young man. And a great many more. If you'd like to come with me, I'll get it for you to read while you're here." Aaron stood up and looked at Logan. "That is if it's okay with your dad."

Logan was distracted. Because if he had been more focused, Aaron was sure he wouldn't have let Matthew go alone with a near stranger. As soon as he picked the boy up he transported them both to within the library of his home. Mathew moved to the wall of books and looked at the titles, careful not to touch them.

"Lizzy likes to read. She said she prefers books over a reading device, though she has one. Do you? Have one of those reader things?"

Mathew nodded.

"Take whatever ones you want and return them when you're finished."

"They're old, aren't they?"

"Yes, they are."

"I bet you have other copies for kids, huh? Why don't you take me to those?"

Aaron sat down and looked around the room. "These are the only books I have, and I trust you with them. If I didn't think you'd take care of them, I would never have suggested you read them. Books are for reading, Mathew, not just to put on display in a nice room."

"My mom has some books. She won't let me touch them. She said they're worth more than me."

Aaron tried to hide his shock that a mother would say such a thing. "What the hell is wrong with her? Who would say such a thing to anyone, much less their own child? Why, I would never have said...that is outrageous, and I think she should be horsewhipped." Aaron looked at Matthew, realizing what he'd said about his mom. But the boy only shook his head when he tried to tell him he was sorry.

"She doesn't like me much. She's never said it, but I can tell. She said she won't marry that man she lives with because my dad won't have to pay her support any more. Lizzy isn't anything like her, is she?"

"No, she's not. And she'd never say anything like that of a child. Children are the most precious things we can create."

Mathew nodded as he touched the binding to the book that they'd been talking about.

"I want you to have that. As a gift."

"I can't take that, Mr. MacManus. I know it's gotta be worth more than me." He touched it again before putting his hands in his pocket. "I really would like to read it if you're sure."

Aaron walked over, took the book from the shelf, and handed it to him. Mathew opened it to the first page carefully and saw the signature on it. He looked up at him. "It's to you."

Aaron nodded with a barely visible hint of a smile.

"You knew him? You met Wyss? He wrote this one book and you have it. That is so cool."

Aaron looked at the other books he had and handed Mathew three more, *The Iliad,* and *The Odyssey* by Homer, *Walden* by Henry David Thoreau, and for a bit of fun, *Bluebeard* by Kurt Vonnegut. They were all signed first editions. They moved back to the castle through the special opening in his office to the delight of the young man.

As Mathew scampered off to read a good book, Aaron looked at Logan as he sat near Lizzy's bed. He wanted to tell him it would be all right, but he stayed away. This was going to have to be something that he worked out on his own. Sara came to sit next to him.

"You bonding with your new grandson?"

He smiled and nodded.

"Lizzy's going to be all right, isn't she, Aaron? I can't lose my little girl."

He pulled her into his arms. "She's here. If she wasn't, things might go differently. Mel said that she's called in the Fates. If Logan doesn't want her, she's going to see if she can get them to break the bond between them so she can live."

"She's given up. That's what this is; she's given up and now she may die."

Aaron thought she was right. He didn't know why Lizzy'd given up, but she had all the same. They both stood up when Logan came into the room.

"I don't love her."

Aaron felt his beast surge with anger.

"But I do like her. She's annoying and bossy and has a mouth that makes me want to sit up and beg, but I don't love her. For now, that has to be enough."

"It will be. For now," said a new voice. They all looked at Elizabeth, Mel's grandmother, as she walked into the room. "Lizzy will not go willingly, young man, nor will she be grateful to you. She's got a stubborn streak in her that I've only encountered once before, and while I love him dearly, I don't like him much."

Elizabeth looked at Aaron, who smiled. She loved him. Grinning like a loon, he told her that he loved her too.

"Tell me what I have to do. And if I have to be converted...I'm not sure. There's my son to think of, and my sister. I can't leave them, so that part of my day I can't be with them."

"That won't be an issue." Elizabeth started toward the bed and Logan with her. "You'll have to feed her. Do you know what that means?"

Her voice faded as they moved away. Aaron stood and watched the two of them together and wondered what the man was going to do when he found out he was nearly all the way to being a vampire anyway.

~~~

Logan took a deep breath. He had to feed her. Then...well, no one knew for sure, but he was willing to bet it was a bit more involved than they'd said. He walked to the bed. He'd been assured she was breathing, but he could barely see her chest rise and fall. Touching her skin, he was amazed at how cold it was. Aaron had told him that it was because her body had shut down in order for it to heal. But she'd gone much deeper than necessary and needed a kick start to come back.

Come back to him.

Aaron's knife, a beautiful bejeweled thing, was in Logan's hands, courtesy of Zane. But before Logan could do anything, that tightening sensation returned, followed by the appearance of yet another beautiful woman.

"Are all super beings lovely, or are you hiding some hideous face that I won't be able to see until this is over?" She laughed, and he flushed. "I'm terribly sorry. I'm shit stupid scared I'm making the biggest mistake of my life."

"I'm Morrigan, the Goddess of all Faeries. Have you heard of me?" He nodded, but then shook his head. "Which is it, child? I'm on a time thing here."

"Heard of you, yes, know who you are, not so much. And just for the record, come earlier if you want to play in my park. I've got my mate to save."

"So you do. But we have time, a little anyway." She sat down on nothing. He watched as she reached out her hand and a glass of blood red wine—maybe it *was* blood —appeared in it.

"It is wine. And before you ask, yes, I read your mind. It's why I'm here. You have questions that haven't been answered. I can answer them. All of them. But you have to give me something in return for each question. A boon, if you may."

Logan was tired of all the games and shit going on that he wasn't getting. He had only had sex with a woman in an elevator and now he had to save her life. This was some major fucked up crap.

"You didn't just have sex with her. You bonded. But that too was planned. You were supposed to meet her some years ago, but wires got crossed and you had the little boy. Great kid, by the way. But you didn't connect." She shifted on her air chair and put her feet up. "So we arranged for you to meet in the hospital."

"You arranged for... My sister and son, you had them nearly killed?" She shook her head. "Then what? If you had anything to do with what happened to them, so help me, I'll rip you apart."

"No, we didn't. You were to meet in the hospital under other circumstances. Mathew was to have fallen at school, nothing major, but our Lizzy would have been there as well when Andi went into labor. When the attempted murder occurred, we simply moved it around so you'd be there together. The elevator stopping was supposed to get you together, but Lizzy was drained from healing the two of them and bit you."

Logan sat down. "She healed them? I don't understand. My sister said she thought Lizzy gave her blood, but Mathew said nothing."

"And he wouldn't have. She used her power to heal him. Had she not, he would have lost both legs to the thigh. The car that ran over him had hit him across both knees and shattered both from there down. She completely healed his right leg and set the other so his leg was broken but not shattered. Lizzy thought it would be hard for him to get around if both were broken." She handed him a small device. "I will tell you what's on that before you look, but it's of your sister's injuries. Her throat had been sliced from ear to ear. Lizzy gave her blood just as your sister said. But she didn't realize that both their bloods were pouring out faster than it was going through Donna's body. Lizzy had to seal the carotid artery so that her blood would heal the other wounds that were draining Donna as well."

Logan put the small laptop thing on the bed. He wasn't sure if he could ever look at them, but knew that right now he could not. He looked at Lizzy lying there so still. "She did save their lives. Both of them."

Morrigan nodded.

"All right. I need questions answered, but I'm not going to give you my left arm or my family. Deal?"

"Deal. And because I owe Lizzy something, I will not charge you for the first three questions. She will be pissy enough when she finds out we've struck a bargain."

He had a feeling he was going to be also. He looked at the woman, then back at Lizzy. He wanted so much information but knew that whatever this woman answered was going to cost. If he saved Lizzy, she'd answer them for him. He looked at Morrigan. "Will I become a vampire?" She only grinned. He wasn't sure what meaning was behind it.

"No. You are one." Her grin widened.

He shook his head.

"You are everything that Lizzy is and more. As she is a day walker, you are as well. She has the power to heal, you do as well. Everything she is, you are also."

She was trying to tell him something. He knew it was right there, but he wasn't getting it. Looking down at Lizzy again, he thought about her healing his son. She'd healed his son. "I can heal her."

The woman applauded, that grin widening further.

With more confidence, he said, "I can heal her as she did Mathew. I don't know how, but I can…the dragon told me that all things are done better when they are done with free will. That's what the other lady said as well. I needed to make Lizzy better, but it had to be freely given."

"Would you like to know how to heal her, Logan? I will tell you for a price."

He shook his head and stood up.

"You will need to know how to heal her, will you not?"

"Yes, I will." Closing his eyes, he thought of the king Shamus and of Aaron, her father. The door opened, and both men stood there while Morrigan smiled.

"You learn fast. But you still have two questions. Shall I bank them for you?" He nodded. "Then I will leave you to your work."

As soon as she was gone, Logan told them what the woman had told him. Then he asked them how it worked. Shamus walked to the bed and put Logan's hand on Lizzy's heart. Then Aaron put his hand over both of theirs.

"Say it, Logan. And it must be freely given."

Nodding, he tried to think what to say. Nothing was coming to mind until he looked at her face. "I, Logan Burris, will you to live. You saved my family at great risk to your own health. You've continued to watch over them even though all I did was shove you away. Even when my household was under attack, you still managed to save us again. I don't love you, Elizabeth MacManus, but I respect you. I may not ever love you, but I admire you. I wish to spend the rest of my days seeing if I can come to love you, so I beg for you to wake up and be pissed at me for doing this."

They all stood very still. Then Shamus laughed, and Aaron joined him. After a few minutes of trying to be mad at them, Logan laughed too. That had to be the worst proposal he'd ever heard.

"Well," Shamus said with a great deal of laughter. "That was freely given, that's for sure. You might want to work on something a little more romantic for when she gets up. Lizzy is a wonderful woman, but she can be a bit on the caustic side."

"And you can't be?" Lizzy's eyes fluttered open as she spoke softly. She cleared her throat as she opened her eyes fully and looked up at him and smiled.

Logan let go of the breath he hadn't known he was holding.

"You're as ass and we both know it. Daddy, tell him so."

Logan leaned down and kissed her. When she wrapped her arms around him, he forgot about the others in the room and started to climb into the bed with her. A clearing of someone's throat had him stop just short of rolling on top of her.

"Would you please wait until I'm out of the room?"

Logan smiled at Aaron, embarrassed.

"She is my daughter, you know, and the thought of you two... I'm out of here. I'm glad you're better, little girl, but even I have to draw the line at this. Shamus, come on."

"But it's just starting to get interesting." Aaron growled and Shamus turned to go after him but stopped. "Lizzy, love, you should know that he's as good at thwarting Morrigan as you are. Nipped her right in the bud." He was laughing when he left the room, closing the door behind him.

Logan took her mouth again and rolled over her to lie beside her. She looked pale, but he knew why now. Logan touched her hair and curled it around his finger as he looked at her. She started to roll away, but he pulled her back.

"What did she take from you?"

"Who?"

"Morrigan. What did you have to give her to make me well again? Whatever it was, I can bargain for its return."

"She gave me three questions to ask, but I only used one. When she offered to tell me how to heal you, I asked for your dad and Shamus to help." She turned to look at him. "She told me that I am everything that you are. So I knew since you healed Mathew, I could heal you."

"You didn't have to do that."

He realized she was right, he didn't. But he'd wanted to. "That's a good point."

"And another thing," he continued, "I have nowhere to live now. Someone burned down my house. They are saying that it was set deliberately. Do you know anything about it?" She turned away without a response, and he pulled her back. "You're going to have to keep me in the loop now. And there will be times when I don't want to know, but you have to tell me, okay?"

She nodded and rolled to her back. He watched the emotions race across her face, and wondered if she knew that he could read her. Frowning, he wondered if he could talk to her through their minds as he had been told all mates could do.

"Yes. Just concentrate on me and the connection will be there. You can read minds too if you're gentle enough. I used to be so horrible at it that I'd hurt people when I did it. Then one day, Sam pushed back at me mentally only about half of what I was doing to her at trampling through her mind. When my mom yelled at her, she gave it all to my mother. After that,

I learned how to do it from Sam until I got better at it than she'd been."

"How many aunts do you have?" She laughed and he smiled. "Do you know that I haven't heard you do that nearly enough? With my son, yes, but not with me."

"I like your kid. He's fun."

He growled at her, leaned in, and nipped gently at her shoulder.

"And he doesn't hog the last of the pancakes."

"Those were delicious. You'll have to make them more often." She looked away, but he pulled her back. "You will stay with me, won't you? Marry me too? I want you to be my wife."

"It's not necessary that we marry, Logan. We're mated, that's enough."

He shook his head. "No, it's not."

"We'll live for a very long time and a marriage isn't necessary. Besides, I have everything I need and—"

"It's necessary to me." He pulled her into his arms to simply hold her. "I'm sorry I hurt you, Lizzy. More than you can know, I'm sorry."

"It's fine, Logan. It was a lot to take in."

He rubbed her back and he felt her relax by degrees. Soon she was limp over him and he felt himself drifting as well. His last thought was that he had to find them a place to live…and soon.

Chapter 7

The house was completely gone. Everything they had owned was either burnt or covered in soot and water. Lizzy picked up a picture frame only to have it fall apart in her hands. She looked up to see where Mathew was and saw him sitting on a stone wall near where his bedroom had been. She looked at Logan, who was talking to the insurance man, and walked over to talk to Mathew.

"All my books are gone."

She nodded and remembered what her dad had told her about lending Mathew books.

"And my stuff. My sheets too, and they were my favorite."

"They were very soft. I would have loved sheets like that." He kicked at something near his foot. "We can see if we can find you more sheets if you want."

He nodded but didn't say anything. She knew some of the things in his room his mom had given him, and there had been things like posters and banners to football games that he and his dad had gone to together. Lizzy tried to think what it would be like to lose all her things but couldn't.

"Do you think we'll build us another house here?" he asked.

"I don't know."

"We could build closer to your mom and dad. And it could be a littler house too. Your dad said I could use his library any time I wanted, and he didn't care if I ate at his desk either."

"That's pretty special. My dad doesn't eat at the desk." Which was true. He couldn't eat anywhere. She nearly giggled at the thought. "Mom and Dad said we could stay with them until we find a place. I guess you wouldn't mind that."

"No way. Your mom is so cool. Did you know she could pull a rabbit out of a hat? And that Duncan can make the best sandwiches in the world? And they have a pool and everything." He glanced at his dad. "Lizzy, I have a question. I heard that lady Mel saying something to Mrs. M, and she said that you and my dad are mates. Does that mean you guys are going steady or something?"

"Something like that. Your dad asked me to marry him. You think that would be okay?" He leapt up and wrapped his arms around her. "I guess you like the idea."

"Yes. Wow, you'd be like my mom, wouldn't you?" She nodded. "And Mr. and Mrs. M would be like my grandparents?"

"Yes, and my brothers would be like your uncles. I take it you're okay with that as well." He nodded, but then frowned. "What is it?" she asked.

"My other mom, she's not going to like this. She says that she'll mess everything up if he thinks he can replace her. I think I know what she means, but… Does she mean she'll try and break you guys up?"

"She can try," Logan said. They both looked at Logan when he spoke. "Mathew, you don't have to worry about your mom. She'll behave or she might get things messed up for her."

Mathew nodded and moved closer to her when his dad sat on the other side. They all watched the insurance adjuster drive away. Logan stretched out his legs before he started talking.

"We're fully covered both here and at my office building. The damage there isn't much, mostly just equipment and a few walls will need to be repaired, but they said it will be covered too. The police have asked them to hold off on repairs, however, until they can investigate who did it." She looked at him and then at Mathew. "The house, of course, is a total loss, and he said that we should be all right if we wanted to look or rebuild right away. So, what are we doing for the rest of the day?"

"House hunting." Mathew made it sound like a death sentence. She laughed and asked him why he hated it so much. "Because they flirt with dad and ignore me. I think I had some good questions too. That other lady? She acted like I was a bug or something."

Lizzy looked at Logan, who was flushing. "Yeah, she did sort of flirt with me. But we got a good house out of the deal."

"Yeah, one that burned down with my favorite sheets in it."

She had to put her hand over her mouth as the two of them argued all the way to the car.

"I don't think her flirting with me is the reason your sheets are gone. It was the fault of some very bad men that I'm going to catch with the help of some of Lizzy's friends." He took her hand as they got to the car. "I guess we'll need a car too. This one is going to be too small for us to shop in."

"I hate shopping too." Mathew looked at them stubbornly. "You are not going to be my dad's wife either. I don't like you at all. I want you to go away and not ever come back here. You're just…stay away from my dad now."

She looked at Mathew and reached out to touch his head to see if he was all right. It wasn't like him to be so mouthy and mean. He flinched from her hand, and she grabbed him and pulled him close. She looked at Logan when she realized what was happening.

"Get in the car," Lizzy ordered. "Now. And drive straight to my parents' house. Someone is trying to get him to come to them by making us send him away. Now, Logan."

He moved to the other side of the car and got in as she held Mathew in the front seat. She had to finally hold him as tightly as she could because he was fighting her so hard. Lizzy reached for her mom with her mind. *"We're nearly there. Someone is screwing around with Mathew. They want him to come to them. I need your help."*

"Calm down," her mother said. *"Look into the boy's eyes. What do you see?"*

"Christ, they're blue. Whoever has him can see us too."

"I'll be out front. The house is safe, so come right in. And for heaven's sake, don't tell Logan where Mathew can hear you."

She told Logan what was going on and what they had to do through their new link. He nodded, but said nothing out loud. She could feel his fear so she reached for his hand. When he took it, she felt his strength as if it were her own.

As soon as they pulled up in front of the house, her mom and Mel came out. Mom hugged her and told her it was a pleasant surprise to see them. Lizzy asked if they could watch Mathew for a little while, saying they could get some house hunting done. Her mom said yes, and they moved to the door. As soon as they were close, Mathew started screaming.

"Get him inside now!"

Logan finally had to take him, and still, the boy fought. As soon as they crossed the threshold, his screaming stopped, and he closed his eyes.

Mel sat with him in her arms for several minutes before she laid him on the couch. She walked into the kitchen with them after asking Duncan to keep an eye on him.

"I shall, my lady. I like the young man. He is ever so polite to me and cleans up after himself very well. His aunt is in residence as well. Shall I ask her to sit with him too?" Mel nodded, and when Duncan left, she sat at the table.

"He'll be fine now. No one will be able to get to him again. And if they try, I'll find her in a heartbeat and make her pay like they won't believe. It's a spell. You were right, Lizzy. Someone wanted him to come to them, and they were getting him to misbehave so that you'd send him to the car alone. I would say they only succeeded as little as they did because he is stronger than they thought and he fought their urge to be bad." Mel looked at Logan as she continued. "I'm sorry, son, but it's his mother. She knows about Lizzy and the money and thinks to blackmail you into giving her more."

"Money? I don't have any more now than when I divorced her two years ago." He looked at Lizzy when Mel did. "She won't hurt you. I'll pay her whatever she wants to make sure of that."

"It's not your money she wants. It's mine. I have a great deal of it. More than you would imagine." He sat down when she asked him to, and he moved to the closest chair and sat, not sure he wanted to hear what she had to say. "My father has a wealthy realm and I have relatives, blood relatives, that have been very generous in my life. Mel has given me more for my birthdays than most people make in a lifetime. And I've invested well."

"I had heard that your parents were worth billions, but there was no mention of you," Logan said, to which she nodded. "It was on purpose then."

"Yes. Your ex-wife must have found out about me. It wouldn't take much to find out. Anyone with enough computer time could have figured it out. And then there's the recent purchase I made of a castle in France."

"You own a castle in France?"

She nodded.

"Okay. Well I... Shit, Liz, I don't know what to say about that."

"Then don't say anything. So if she knows that, it's a safe bet she knows everything." He nodded. "Logan, she has help from some powerful beings. Do you know who it might be?"

She watched him as he seemed to think on it. He pulled out his cell phone and thumbed through it, then handed it to her. She didn't know the name and handed it to her mom and Mel.

"Black Magic? How original. May I call them?"

Logan nodded at Mel. She pressed the button and waited. When she disconnected the call and handed it back to him, she looked grim.

"What is it?" Lizzy asked her. "You can't just call them and say nothing. Damn it, this concerns my son." She flushed when she realized what she said and turned to Logan to apologize. He was grinning at her. When he pulled her into his arms, she felt like she'd come home. Mel cleared her throat.

"It's Megan Sims."

Lizzy pulled away.

"I'd recognize that whiny nasal voice anywhere. She answered by saying she was the owner."

"Good Christ," her mom said. "I thought she was dead."

~~~

"We let a few children come to some of these classes that we held at the castle. Lizzy, of course, came, as did Mac and a few of the other beings' children were invited as well. Most of them had a little power, but none as much as Lizzy and Mac. When Megan showed up the first day, she picked a fight with Mac." Mel smiled at him. "Lizzy has always been overly protective of Mac, but this time, she nearly got her ass handed to her."

"She cheated."

Logan looked at Lizzy.

"She used magic and we weren't supposed to. Not until we learned how to do it safely. She used it to try and hurt me."

Sara laughed. "She got her back, though. The next day, Megan tried the same thing, and she ended up with a bloodied nose and a broken wrist."

Logan looked at Lizzy. "You cheated?" She shook her head and looked at her mom. Logan did too when she laughed again.

"Her uncle Colin showed her how to fight. And him being a big Irishman with an Irishman's temper, he showed her how to fight dirty, but without magic." Sara took his hand and showed him how she'd held her fist. "As soon as her fist connected with Megan, Megan tumbled over her head and ass three times before she fell in the pool. Two of the royal guards could hardly get her out they were laughing so hard."

"So she came back and learned to play with magic, and now she's using it against you?" He was confused by them all shaking their heads. "You said she had classes with Lizzy. I don't understand."

"Lizzy uses white magic, as do the rest of us. Megan's is black." Mel picked up the small herb in the pot in the window and brought it to the table. "This herb is a pot of white magic, say. And the roots go deep into the soil and it grows. When the plant has served its purpose, someone here will pull it out of the soil and cut it up and put it back into the dirt. The soil then is repaid for what it gave the user. Understand?"

Logan nodded. "Sort of like recycling of plastic bags that they make benches out of. Reusable and recycled."

"Sort of, but the plant that died actually helps the next plant grown in this pot." Lizzy took a bowl from the sink, brought it to the table, and poured some of the dirt into it as she continued with Mel's explanation. "This is the same dirt, same dead plant, and the same user. But this time, instead of putting the dead plant in, the earth takes it and prolongs its life by using magic. Any person using black magic hasn't borrowed from the earth but has actually stolen from it. He's tainted the earth. And in doing so, he's stained this area and nothing will grow here. Anything within this area will have to take from things that are close until after a while, instead of a small area poisoned, the area is completely dead."

He looked at the dirt as he tried to think what they were telling him. "So anyone who uses black magic can't renew their own resources and they take from others. And in doing so, make a bigger stain on themselves and others. This goes on until they have to move on and take from somewhere else."

"That's it exactly." Mel nodded and put the plant back, as well as the bowl. "But even if you only use white magic, or pure magic, you must remember to pay back whatever you borrow from. Lizzy gets her power from the earth, as does her mom. I get mine from everywhere, but mostly from the castle and the kingdom. Shamus does as well. But the person who is trying to harm you gets it from the darker things and steals it from others because she can no longer make it herself. She has to steal from others, making hers blacker still."

"And what happens to the earth? Where she would have gotten her black magic in the first place?" He looked at Mel when Lizzy did. "It's dead, right? It can never be used again."

"Right. The stronger she gets, the darker her magic, the more things around her will die. Including herself. That's why she'll steal more, not just to be more powerful, but to sustain her own life." Lizzy sat down next to him and touched his forehead. "You have to work on what you have."

He nodded. "Tell me what I have to do. I want to know so that when she tries to hurt my son... How did you know?"

Lizzy smiled. "He was so negative. Usually, he's so up and happy that he makes me feel that way simply by being with him. But today, it was as if he found fault with everything. Including the new house."

"And that made you touch his mind?"

She nodded.

"I want to learn to do that first. It might come in handy. And I can talk to you without anyone knowing what we're saying, right? Like we did in the car when you told me what was going on."

"See what else you can do? You can touch me as well."

When he felt Lizzy brush against his cheek, his cock leapt. She was sending him images that were so erotic that he nearly stood up to take her to the bedroom. *"Would you like me to suck your cock, Logan? Take you deep into my mouth and fondle your balls?"*

He nodded but didn't move. *"Can we come this way? Can we have sex without actually touching each other?"* She nodded.

"But first I want you to move this knife," she said. He looked down at the one that appeared on the table. *"Move it from here to the sink for me."*

A knife on the table moved just a little then it seemed to take flight. Aaron walked in just as it flew through the air, and had it not been for his quick reflexes, he might have been hurt.

"Working on some of our skills, are we?" Aaron sat down as he continued. "Did you know that Mathew is in the game room with Duncan? They're playing a very heated game that Tristan left here. I have no idea what it's called."

Logan didn't even ask how this Tristan was related. Everyone he met was either an aunt or an uncle. Lizzy smiled and told him it was a kid's game, as that was all that Tristan made.

The phone ringing startled everyone, and when Lizzy reached for it, he laughed when her dad smacked her hand. It was his home, he told her. But the moment he said hello, Logan knew that something was wrong. He looked at him as he talked to the person on the other end.

"Yes, I know who Logan Burris is. No, I don't believe I will. Well, if that's the way you…" The long pause made Aaron angry so much so that his eyes turned that dark red again. "We shall see, won't we, and in the meantime, I'd like to tell you something. When you fuck with one of mine, you fuck with me. And when you do that, know that I come with a great deal more power behind me than your average vampire. You should call the Council and ask them about pissing in my sandbox."

Aaron hung up the phone and held up his hand when Lizzy started to ask him who it had been. When Mathew walked in the room, Logan nearly reached for him to keep him out of harm's way.

"Hey, Grandpa, come and play some Collect the Money with me."

Aaron seemed to melt before his eyes as he stared at Mathew.

"Dad and Lizzy said it would be okay if I called you that, right?"

"It's perfect, and your timing couldn't have been planned better. Thank you." As Aaron walked by him, he reached out and hugged him. "Thank you for the greatest gift a man could ask for from his children. Someone to call him grandpa."

CHAPTER 8

Megan tried to find the number on the Internet, as well as the reverse directory that she'd paid fifty dollars for. Nothing. The only person she could think it would have been who'd called yesterday and hung up was her sister. She was forever borrowing someone's phone and not leaving a message when Megan didn't answer. But this person had called her business and Megan had answered it.

"You have any of that stuff that'll make your hair grow?"

Megan looked at the woman who had been in here for over an hour asking the most ridiculous questions. Most of which she'd answered, "No, we're not that kind of shop." But she kept asking. "I don't know what you mean. You want your hair to grow longer?" The woman nodded and Megan mentally rolled her eyes. "Yes, here it is."

She handed her a bottle of wart removal and went back to the counter to check to see if anything on the number had popped up yet. Still searching was the story of her life. She looked down at the newspaper clipping she'd found this morning.

"Millionaire Logan Burris to wed Elizabeth MacManus." First he tries to take her building from her, and now he was marrying the bane of her existence. Lizzy had been making her life hell since she'd met her over seventy years ago. She looked up as the woman asked another question.

"You carry any of those candles?"

Megan looked around the room at the nearly four dozen candles she had out on display.

"Not those. The kind that will transport you to other realms."

Megan stared at her for a long moment, wondering if anyone would miss her if she were to suddenly disappear. Coming around the corner of her counter, she went to the door and told the woman it was time to go.

"But your sign says five o'clock. It's not even three yet."

Megan looked at her watch and groaned. She didn't care if it was noon; she was closing up. "It's closing time now. I have a batch of 'grow a second head' brewing in the back and it's about ready to come out of the pot." The woman stared at her for several seconds and Megan felt a shiver of fear roll down her back. "You'll need to leave now."

The woman nodded and turned to leave. But not before falling into her and nearly knocking them both to the floor. She was gone before Megan could hurt her for being so stupid. She was locking the door when she realized that her things were still on the counter and hadn't been paid for.

She couldn't afford this much longer. This store front was draining her resources. If she didn't have to pay rent for this building, she'd be fine, but her landlord, a greedy prick, had decided six months ago that if she was going to live there and have a shop, he should get three times the amount. It still made no sense to her, but according to the free advice she got on one of those hotlines about rights, they said it was his building and she had no lease. But if she wanted to take him to court for a small fee of ten thousand dollars, they'd represent her.

"If I had that sort of money, I'd just buy the building next door and move in." Only now she couldn't because Burris had decided that he wanted it and had offered twice that. "Fucking rich bastard."

She looked at the paper again and wondered why he was marrying Lizzy and if he knew what she was. Probably. Vampires needed sex like they needed blood and she would have taken a hunk out of him by now. Megan ran her finger down Logan's cheek in the picture.

Handsome didn't begin to describe the man. Dark hair and the greenest eyes she'd ever seen on anything. She knew the kid had them too, and she had tried to change her eyes to match. All she'd managed to do was make herself blind for several hours. No matter what the magic, you couldn't make a permanent change to your own body that others would recognize. It was forbidden.

"And because the queen says so then it has to be a fact." Megan went about her business of closing up her shop and making sure that things were where they were supposed to be. She did find an odd item among the things that the woman had had.

It was a pretty green bottle with a cork in it. It appeared to be empty, so she opened it and sniffed to see if there was odor in it in the event she wanted to use it for something. But as it looked, it was devoid of smells as well. Putting it into her pocket, she took it upstairs with her along with the newspaper.

The news on the television had a small snippet about Logan's house burning down, which she watched. The man had driven her to this. As well as a little something about the break-in at the building he worked in. The news anchor had said that the two were unrelated.

Unrelated? How was that possible? She'd had them done on the same day by the same group of wolves. They had been instructed to make it look like a murder, but had found no one in either building. It was actually her that had ended up burning down the house, as her anger had gotten the best of her. Damn it all to hell. Unrelated?

After making her a light dinner of salad and boiled eggs, she went to the basement of her building. She unlocked the door to the little room she'd built, walked in, and sat down on the chair. The woman there looked up, but she didn't speak to her.

"It'll do you no good not to talk to me. I've proven to you over and over that I'm going to get the information I need whether you give it to me or not." The woman flinched when Megan reached out to touch her. "You're afraid of me. Good. Now tell me what your ex-husband fears the most. And don't tell me it's about the brat. He's too smart for his own good, and I can't make him do what I want this far from him."

She didn't move. Megan was sort of glad she didn't talk. She had a voice that would cut through steel and leave it sharp and jagged. Even her memories were hard to take at times. She was the most annoying person she knew and would lie about everything. Actually, Megan thought that a good trait as long as she didn't lie to her. That pissed her off.

"Tight places. Especially in the dark."

The information was freely given and Megan didn't trust it. So she reached into the woman's mind and raped it. There was so much useless crap that it took her several minutes to find it. By the time she was finished, the woman's nose was bleeding and she hung limply in the chains that held her to the wall. Megan figured she would last another couple of days, but not much longer than that.

That didn't bother Megan other than the fact that she'd have to figure out what to do with the carcass. Over the decades she'd been alive, it was getting harder and harder to find places to hide the bodies. And with technology so behind in this world, she couldn't find a way to rid herself of them out in cyberspace either.

It was time to pay her little buddies a visit. Especially Lizzy. That woman had been a pain in her ass since she'd bloodied her nose when they'd been ten. And she'd never been able to get her mind to wrap around the fact that she'd not used magic to best her. The fucking bitch was going to pay.

~~~

The house was perfect. As Lizzy walked from one room to the next, she marveled at the sheer size of it, as well as how well it had been maintained. The house was as old as her parents' house, but this one had sublevels that the realtor hadn't understood. She'd told her and Logan that the previous owners must have had a real fear of the end of the world.

"The rooms are set up with locks on the inside. There are bathrooms in each room as well as a small kitchenette. They had to think they'd be down here for a while and wanted to be able to sustain themselves."

Lizzy smiled and looked at Logan. *What they really wanted to do was come down here and not be killed from the sun.* She spoke to Logan through their connection so he'd get used to it. *Of course, being a human, she wouldn't know that.*

"Lizzy, I want you."

She turned to look at him.

"Right now, I want to fuck you so badly that my cock hurts. Send her away and I'll make it worth your while."

The woman left the room without a word, and Lizzy locked the door from where she was. Logan walked to her and she felt her body respond to his like he was already touching her.

"You mentioned sucking my cock."

She nodded and reached out to run her hand up his thigh to his hard shaft.

"I want you to undress me and take me into your mouth."

Lizzy unsnapped his jeans and slowly lowered his zipper. She watched his face, waiting for some sign that she was doing something he liked. When she had his pants opened, she reached into them and cupped him through his boxers. He moaned and rocked into her hand.

Moving down on her knees, she pulled his jeans down until they were to his knees and reached up to pull his boxers off. His cock was already thick and leaking at the tip, and she licked the tiny pearl off.

"Run your tongue around the crown, then along the length."

She did as he instructed, then suckled on the dark head.

"Christ, baby, that's it."

Learning him was delicious. Every time she tasted more of him on her tongue, she found she wanted more. When he curled his fingers into her hair, she looked up at him and saw that he had his eyes closed and he was breathing hard. She reached into his mind and let him feel what she was feeling. He looked down at her.

"Can I do that?" She nodded. It took him a few seconds, but once he figured out how to do it, she was flooded with him. Images began to hit her. Him coming over her body, her riding his mouth as he ate her. Even as she tried to sort them, he sent her more and more until she was sliding her fingers down to her pussy.

He stepped back and she reached for him. His cock was wet from her mouth, and his precum was in a long stream from the tip. Licking her lips, she moved toward him and he told her to stop.

"The floor. I want you on the floor so I can eat you. I need to taste you before I come inside of that sweet pussy."

She stood and stripped quickly, leaving a trail of her clothes as she tossed them from her. As soon as she was naked, he told her to lie down.

He stood over her for several seconds before he spoke again. "You look like a feast. Something that I can gorge myself on for months and never get enough. Open your legs for me. I want to see how wet you are."

She spread her legs for him and bent her knees up. He moaned and got down on his knees. As soon as he rolled to his back, she sat up and looked at him.

"You're going to ride my mouth," he said. "I've wanted you to do that for weeks now, but every time I'm near you all I can think about is being inside of you. Come here."

She moved over his chest and he told her to turn around. Now she could see the advantage of being in this position. His cock was right in front of her. Leaning down, she took him into her mouth and nearly screamed when he pulled her down and suckled her clit.

Lizzy experimented with him, learning what made him come up off the floor deeper into her mouth to what made his cock leak more. Every time he nipped at her, she'd nip back. Her fangs dropped and she ran them along his thigh to feel him shudder beneath her. When she felt his mouth at the vein in her thigh, she reached to him and told him to think of biting her, sinking his teeth into her and drinking from her. She found his own vein in his leg and licked along it. Wrapping her hand around his cock, she sank her fangs into his leg and fisted his cock. He came hard and quick, his body jerking hers so hard that he nearly bucked her off. Then she screamed.

He'd bitten her, and her climax, close to the edge already, detonated around her, sizzling her blood in her body and making her want more. Sealing the tiny wound, she took his cock into her mouth and sucked his cum from him, filling her body as he took from her.

Lifting her head from him, she rolled off and to her hands and knees. He came up behind her and slammed into her. His hands at her hips dug deeply into her, leaving marks she knew would be gone long before the memory of what he was doing to her ever faded. Leaning over her, pressing her head to the floor, he took her like an animal.

"Please. I need to come again." He growled and she felt her body tighten. When he bit her shoulder, she cried out and reached between her legs to her pussy. He stopped her with another low growl. "Then help me, damn it." He chuckled against her shoulder and released her flesh. As soon as he sat up, she rolled to her back, and he was deep inside of her again, his mouth at her breast.

"Come. Come now and bring me with you." His command, full of compulsion, took her quickly. Tightening her body around his as she came, she felt the moment he came too. He took her throat as she sank her fangs deep into his wrist he'd offered her.

Lizzy couldn't move and it had little to do with the man lying over her. When he'd dropped onto her, she had felt as weak as he had seemed to be. When he lifted his head and rested it on his fisted hand, she smiled at him.

"We should probably go and find the realtor."

She shook her head and told him she'd sent her home.

"Good, but how do we make an offer on the house if she's not here to take it?"

"I hadn't thought of that. When you told me to get rid of her, I did." He rolled off her and stood, helping her up as she continued. "I was thinking we'd have my dad buy the house for us. That way there's no trace to us if Megan decides to come after this one."

She was pulling on her jeans when he came up behind her and spoke close to her ear. "If you'd like. But before we move in, your dad said he'd send a security crew to the house and have it set up for us. He said he has the best there is."

She nodded and turned in his arms. He was beautiful, and his eyes were so gorgeous that she wanted to sink into them. When he kissed her on the mouth and pulled back to finish dressing, she told him what the house was going to need in addition to the security.

"My dad can't take the full sun. Most of it, but not all. I'd like to have shades like his put over the house. They also act as an extra security measure." She looked at him when he didn't answer. He was standing perfectly still with his pants halfway up his body and his shirt still undone.

"I bit you."

She nodded, smiling.

"I mean not just a nibble on your skin like I love to do, but actually sank my…" He moved to the bathroom and stared in the mirror. She came in behind him and wrapped her arms around his waist.

"Think of them." She knew the moment that his fangs appeared. "Now do the same to make them shorten again. And try not to run your tongue over them. It'll be hard at first, but you'll get the hang of it."

"Will I need to drink blood too?" She shook her head and told him no. "But then why are they here? Unless it's to bring you pleasure."

"Mostly, yes. Did you enjoy biting me?" He turned to her and pulled her tight against his body. She waited for him to answer, and when he didn't, she looked up at him.

"I was trying to think of a word to describe how incredible it felt. How much I enjoyed tasting your blood in my mouth." He looked down at her. "All I can come up with is fucking wow."

She laughed and hugged him before stepping back. They finished dressing, and as they were leaving the house, he pulled out his phone, called her dad, and asked him to make an offer on the house. He laughed and told him he would have to think on it.

When they got into the car, Logan turned to her. "Your dad asked me if I'd pledge to him. I told him I'd think about it. I honestly didn't say yes because I have no clue what it means."

"A Pledge of Alliance. It means that he'll be your master in all things and you'll pay him a percentage of what you make. Being my mate now, you won't have to pay him anything, but the other is true. You won't be able to buy or sell without his permission, taking a mate if you don't already have one must be cleared through him, as well as any investments. In return, he'll protect you."

"I thought that's what you did?"

She smiled at his joke and told him the rest. Her dad was one ass-kicking vamp. "Dad has more magic and more power than vamps twice his age. He can summon an army with a single thought and he can destroy with a flick of his finger. And I mean destroy whole cities. He would never do that, but he is powerful. My mom is a cousin to the queen, as you know, but she has magic within her that is scary. If I had to go to war, I would want them on my side. If they were the enemy I was against, I'd surrender. Because, as giving and loving as they are, they are ruthless when it comes to justice and fairness to others. And they will kill for what they consider theirs."

"And Mathew and me? How do we fit in the family? I know your dad gets a kick out of Mathew calling him Grandda, but what about when Mac's baby is born. Then what?"

"Nothing will change. I think my dad has been looking forward to someone calling him Grandda more than he'd been looking forward to being called Dad. He is more alive than I've ever seen him."

Her cell was ringing as they pulled in front of the house. She answered it with a smile, wondering what Mac had done to piss off Andi. She answered the phone, asking him what he'd done now.

"It's time. The baby is…Christ, she hurts so much, and I just want to kill someone. Come here now so I don't try to hurt him again."

She laughed and told Logan to wait.

"I'm serious, Lizzy. Thomas said if I touch him again, he's going to stop helping bring him into the world and leave him there. Andi said if he did, I'd never touch her again."

"We're coming now. Have you called Mom and Dad? And can we bring Mathew?"

"Yes, I called him. All Dad did was laugh at me. I told him to stay home and I called you." Lizzy laughed again. "If that's all you're going to do, then you stay home too."

Putting her phone in her pocket after Mac hung up on her, she told Logan what was going on. Her parents and Mathew were racing out of the house as they were reaching for the door. Duncan was close behind them.

"A baby. They're gonna have a baby and we'll get to be the first people in the world to see it." Mathew's excitement was contagious and she laughed too. Fifteen minutes later, they were pulling into Mac's driveway.

Chapter 9

Sara looked around the room. There were more beings here than she'd seen at the castle in months. She smiled when she thought about why they were here. Mac, their little boy, was having a baby. She glanced up at Aaron when he paced by her again.

"If you don't sit down, I'm going to stake you." He snorted but didn't stop. "I mean it, Aaron, you're making the very nice people here very nervous. Sit down."

"Why is it taking so long? I mean, you only took, what, three minutes? We've been here for hours."

She rolled her eyes and looked at her watch. "We've been here for barely one, and it did not take three minutes. You were only there for three minutes. If I remember correctly, you only showed up at the end after I'd been dealing with labor for hours."

He sat next to her and kissed her on the nose. "You didn't feel a thing and you know it. Pete took all your pain and put it aside. And I couldn't be there because it was the hottest part of the day and—"

"You two sound like my mom and dad used to. Do you fight all the time?"

Sara snapped her mouth closed and looked at Mathew.

"It's hard to hear Mr. Draco tell me about flying if you two are gonna fight."

"You're right, my man. And Draco has been around for a long time, so he should have some amazing stories. But Sara and I aren't fighting. We're remembering loudly."

Mathew rolled his eyes much like Sara had done at Aaron.

"She's trying to tell me that I'm wrong. We both know that can't be true now, can it?"

Mathew looked between the two of them before shaking his head. "You two are weird. I love you, but you're very weird."

He walked away, and Sara couldn't breathe. When Aaron took her hand, she looked at him. He was smiling and nodded at her. "Feels good, doesn't it?"

She nodded.

"I would never have guessed that having a little boy tell me he loves me would feel so damned wonderful. And he doesn't have to either. We're nothing more to him than anyone else is in the family, yet he does."

"I don't even care that he thinks we're weird." She looked at Mathew sitting at the feet of the only dragon left in the world and enjoying himself. "He's going to figure this all out soon if he hasn't already. Figure out that we're not as normal as he thinks we all are."

"I think he knows something is different about us. He already knows about the castle and the beings there. He knows that I rest during the day, but can talk to him if he wants." She looked at him, surprised. "He can talk to me on a wavelength that was never there before. A path that I know just he and I share. You should try it. It's amazing."

She reached for his mind and felt the instant connection. When he turned to her and smiled, she wanted to get up and go to him, but he turned back to Draco and spoke to her.

"You're being weird again."

Sara burst out laughing and felt tears gather in her eyes. He was so amazing she wanted to find his dad and hug him.

Standing, she decided to do just that. Sara found him on the deck on the phone.

He glanced at her, but she could tell he was upset. She noticed that Lizzy was seated at the patio table and she too looked upset. She sat with her and waited for Logan to disconnect before she asked what was wrong.

"The realtor. She said that the house we wanted is sold. I've been trying to get him to tell me who bought it for the last ten minutes. Did they say anything when Aaron called them?"

Sara nodded and called Aaron to her.

"We really loved that house, and Mathew was going to be so close to you guys, something he had requested before we left."

Aaron came out the door and she told him what had happened. He nodded and asked Logan to sit. Sara went to stand next to Aaron when he reached for her hand.

"It's our wedding gift to you."

Logan look confused, but Lizzy smiled.

"We actually bought it several years ago and had only had the realtor show you today so we could see if you liked it. When you called me today to ask me to make an offer, we meant to tell you when you got back home, but then Mac called and things—"

"You bought us a house several years ago?"

Sara shook her head at Logan's question and knelt before him to answer him. He looked a little freaked out. "We bought the house for Lizzy to use. Someday we hoped she'd find a mate, but we wanted her to be close to us before she moved far away and never returned. She had started getting restless about then and we were afraid. We never thought of it after she moved in with us as anything but an investment. We had it brought up to its original standards when we bought it."

Logan kissed her on the forehead and nearly fell back in his chair when Aaron growled. She turned to look at him and glared. She could feel Logan's fear and told Aaron to behave.

"Never touch another vampire's mate," Lizzy said.

Sara laughed at the look on Logan's face as he nodded to Lizzy.

"It's sort of a death wish, if you know what I mean. Usually, family doesn't matter, but Dad always has been a bit on the abnormal side."

"I am not. What is it with you younger people? Abnormal indeed. How would you like it if someone ran their hands all over Logan? Would you be so calm about it? Would you—"

The door opened and Mathew was suddenly there. Each of them took a step forward, and Sara pulled a sword from the air. Mathew took a step back.

"I just wanted to tell you the baby is born and Mac is looking for you." He took one more step back before he stiffened and moved forward again. "I was wrong about you guys being weird. You're insane and too tense. Get a massage or something."

He left them there as he tore back into the house. Sara looked at her mate and ran to his arms. The baby was here. They all ran into the house and to the master bedroom. Mac stood up when they came in and looked down at his mate.

"We were beginning to think you didn't care," Andi said, handing the small bundle in her arms to Mac just as Duncan and Mel walked in. Sara was so excited she could hardly breathe. They had been planning this for months. And Mac held his child close as he looked at them all.

"A few months ago, we told you that we had a name for our child and wasn't going to tell anyone until he was born. We were asked to do this by someone very near and dear to us." Mac moved forward as he pealed the blanket opening, revealing the baby within. "Naming him was an honor. Especially for as much as he's done for us over our many lifetimes."

Mac handed his son to Duncan. He looked so confused that Mac had to help him hold him. He looked up at Mac. "I do not understand, Master Mac. Shall I take him below for the others to meet before your parents do?"

Mac shook his head. "No, Duncan, he needs to meet you first. His name is Duncan. Duncan Aaron MacManus, and he's been waiting a long time to tell you that."

Duncan looked at the baby in his arms, then back at Mac. He smiled. "You have named your son for me? Oh, Master Mac, I do not know what... A person named for me is a great honor. Are you sure that is what you... I will not allow you to change it now even if I have to... Oh my, a child." He sat down in the chair nearest him and began to pull all the blankets off so they could see him. When he started to protest that Sara and Aaron should have him, they told him to hold him, they would get their turn. Gently, he pulled the last blanket off.

He was perfect. Dark hair like Mac's covered his tiny head, and his skin looked as soft as down. When Duncan ran his finger down his cheek, the baby opened his eyes and looked right at him. Sara held her breath as they stared at one another.

"You and I are going to have a grand time, young man. I shall tell you stories of your father that will curl your hair. He was not as saintly as his mother thinks."

Mac laughed.

"And do not let that mother of yours fool you. I have some stories of her as well. But for now, you must meet your new family."

Duncan stood and handed her the baby. He even told her to be careful of his little head. She laughed and told him she would be especially careful as she showed him to Aaron. They fell in love instantly.

~~~

Mathew moved to the game room again and picked up the controller. He was playing one of the games when a man came in to sit down in the chair next to him. Mathew tried to ignore him, but he just kept staring. He finally paused the game and looked at him.

"You don't like babies?"

Mathew shrugged.

"I have five. All little girls. Well, not so little any longer, but I have them. You'll have to meet them."

"Thanks. Why are you down here and not up with the new kid?" He flushed when the man laughed. "I didn't mean that. It's just everybody here is related to him and I figured you all would be up there."

Mathew played with the controller in his hand when the man spoke again. "You like this game? I never really cared for it much, but everyone seemed to enjoy it."

"It's okay. The graphics are good, but the game is sort of lame." Mathew looked at the man. "You're Tristan St. James, huh?"

"Yes. And you're Mathew Burris. I'm pleased to meet you." Mathew put the controller down on the table and started for the door. "Are we finished talking?"

Matthew stopped just before leaving the room and turned to the man he'd just insulted. "I just said your game is lame. I wouldn't want to talk to me anymore."

Tristan got up. "I didn't mean to upset you. Come on back and show me how you came to the conclusion that it was lame. I sincerely want to know. It's actually important that I know."

"Why? You probably know this game better than anybody."

"Probably, but this game was written some years ago. See the little girl? That's Lizzy. And the little boy is Mac. I wrote this one when I was staying here when...well, I was doing a favor for someone. But I met my mate so it turned out well."

He hesitated. This man was big, much bigger than his dad, but not fat. He wasn't scary, but he was a stranger. There was something else about him that Mathew had noticed about all the other people around here today. "Can I ask you a question?"

Tristan nodded.

"What are you?"

Tristan leaned back and looked at him. Mathew waited for him to tell him he was just a man, and he knew that would be a lie. He wasn't sure what they all were, but they weren't human.

"I have to ask you something before I tell you. And it's huge, Mathew, something that I've never asked of anyone before." Mathew nodded. "Can you keep a secret no matter what?"

"You mean if they tear my fingernails out and dip me in boiling oil kind of secret?"

Tristan didn't laugh at him, but nodded.

"I can do that. I can keep the best kind of secrets."

"I'm a vampire."

Mathew sat down on the couch and stared.

"So is Aaron and most of the other men in this house right now."

"But not the ladies?"

Tristan told him that some of them were because they'd been changed. But a couple of the women, his mate included, had been made also, but not by a person. They were special. He said that Lizzy was more than that. "I'm a pureblood. Do you know what that is?"

Mathew nodded but then shook his head.

"It means that both my parents are vampires and their parents before them all the way back through our history. Lizzy is more than that. Her dad is a made vampire, meaning that someone converted him, but he's really old, nearly two thousand years old, and Sara is a powerful person because her cousin Mel, you've met her, she's the queen of all magic. Mel's brother is Sara's dad."

"So will Lizzy change my dad into what she is?"

Tristan hesitated.

"She's already done it, hasn't she?"

"I don't think she meant to. I think it just happened. But your dad isn't going to leave you or hurt you."

"I know that." Mathew stared at the paused television. "But someday he and Lizzy will have their own baby and I won't be needed because I'm not like them."

"What balderdash."

Tristan stood and bowed before the woman who came in the room with them. Mathew did as well, not sure he'd ever met this lady before. And Mathew was positive that he'd remember her.

"Lady Elizabeth, I don't think you've met Lizzy's son, Mathew. Mathew, this is the Lady Elizabeth, grandmother to Mel and the first queen of magic."

Not sure what to do, he bowed too. "I'm not really her son. I'm my dad's son, but Lizzy and my dad are...I think he said mates. They're mates." The lady looked at him like he was a bug pinned to a wall. He sort of felt like one too. She turned to Tristan and told him to get them something to drink and to leave them alone. He nodded and left, but not before winking at him.

"You're her son as much as that baby upstairs belongs to Mac. Sit."

He did so and sat up straighter on the couch.

"What sort of person do you think I am?"

"Scary." He put his hand over his mouth, embarrassed that he'd said the first thing that had come to mind. She laughed, but he didn't relax; she really was a little scary.

"When I was made...not made, created, I was an adult. I had no parents, nor did I have anyone to show me the ways of the world. Of course it was much smaller then, less people, no planes or cars. They were still setting about this world in ships and walking everywhere. So I created Avalone. It was a place for me to go and practice my magic. And out of that the Tree of Life was made. Have you seen it when you went to the castle?"

"No, ma'am. I saw a dragon, but we were only there for a little while. And Miss Tess said that they didn't like humans running around without someone to watch over them." She nodded. "I guess I'll never see the tree."

"Next time you come, I'll show it to you. In fact, you and I will take a tour. But I digress."

Tristan returned, handed her a glass, and gave Mathew a soda. He sat it on the table without touching it. He wasn't allowed pop of any kind at any time.

"You don't like it?"

Mathew shrugged at her.

"Ah. He won't allow it. Smart man, your father. Good. What would you like? I can get you whatever you want."

"I like orange juice please." He looked at the bottle he'd put on the table when she nodded to it. "It's juice."

"That's what you wanted, wasn't it?"

He nodded and grinned at her.

"You're easy to please. Anyway, I was created, and my mate was a man who was guard to me. He and I fell in love and had a baby. Then that baby grew up and had one of her own until we got all the way to Lizzy. And now we have you."

"But Lizzy didn't have me. She's not my mom." He thought of her more than his mom sometimes, but she wasn't ever going to be. He looked up at her when she laughed.

"That's what makes you her son. You don't get to pick your family usually, but sometimes one picks you and you're happier for it. That little boy upstairs is your cousin as much as any other baby that come along after you. And those will be your younger brothers and sister as much as you are theirs. None of them will be human, some will be something like their mom, and others will be like their grandda, but none of them will ever be more than you. Do you know why?"

He shook his head.

"Because none of them were the first to see everything you get to see today and beyond."

"So I can tell them everything they missed being born after me?"

She nodded.

"I should take notes for them. Keep them...I have a camera. I could take pictures too and keep them."

"That would be lovely. I think you should have a great camera. I would hate for you to miss something. And you should talk to my mate. He would be your great-great...well, you can call him Grandda too. He has been the keeper of information since I've known him. He can show you how to keep good records."

Excited now, he and Lady Elizabeth, Grams he'd decided to call her, went up to see the new baby. Lizzy hugged him to her, and he felt so loved he nearly burst from it. When Mac asked him if he wanted to hold his son, Mathew nearly went cross-eyed with happiness. He sat on the edge of the bed and held the little guy on his lap.

"I'm going to tell you about today as soon as you get big enough. And I'm going to take your picture all the time." A light flashing made him look up, and Phillip, Elizabeth's mate, had taken his picture. "See, little Dunc, it's starting already."

CHAPTER 10

"I don't really care what you think. In fact, don't do it again. Thinking is bad for your health." Megan glared at the two men in front of her. "Where are they living if not in the mansion? That should be simple enough, don't you think? They have to be staying somewhere, and we all know it's not at the castle. Logan is human. Humans don't live at the castle."

"But they aren't around here either. They were at that house that has the new one, the baby vamp in it. We couldn't get in there, not with all those others around."

She'd heard about the new baby. Everyone who had come into her shop had mentioned it. She was frankly sick to death of the baby and it was less than two days old.

"Well, keep looking. I need for you to bring me Logan within the next couple of days. The sale is supposed to go through in four, and I have to make him understand that he can't just buy what's mine."

And if that didn't work, he would just not be around to make the sale. She started for the stairs to go and talk with Lula again, but got sidetracked when someone came into her shop.

She was really sick of people coming in and telling her they were "just looking around." Looking around at what? The place was one room, and even that was small compared to what she really wanted to do. Why did it take them so fucking long just to look? Buy something and she wouldn't care if the person looked for months.

It was nearly seven hours later before she was able to get to her prisoner. And by the time she got down there, she was dead. Fuck. Now she had no bargaining chip to make Logan do what she wanted. Looking at the dead woman, she wondered what to do with her and decided that putting her in the dumpster across town was her best bet. Even if someone found her, they'd not know who she was. Not unless they had some dental records, of course.

Megan put her in the shower curtain that she'd found on sale a few weeks ago just for this purpose. She had hoped that she'd live a little longer, might have too if she had maybe taken better care of her, but Megan had a life to live too, and taking care of a stupid woman who'd been dumb enough to get caught wasn't her problem.

Loading her in the back of her truck wasn't a big deal. The neighbors were used to seeing her moving crap in and out of the building and would more than likely think that it was just more of the same. She was pulling out of the lot behind the house when she turned and something cut into her leg. Looking down at the blood on her thigh, she got out and reached into her pocket.

The green bottle from yesterday had shattered. Megan went back into the building, stripped off her pants, and put on fresh ones. She hated going to the Laundromat and tried to wear her jeans a couple of times before she had to wash them. Now she'd have to figure out how to get blood out of her pants or buy new ones. Megan stomped out to the truck, pissed more about the jeans than she was about Lula dying. She thought of her parents and wished she had a way of going back in time and asking them why they'd done this to her. Why they hadn't stood up to the queen and demanded to stay in Molavonta where she could grow and have all the things that Lizzy had.

She'd been fifteen when her mother had been called to the throne room. Megan had been told to stay away from the proceedings, but she had snuck in the room and hid behind the curtains. But there were several others ahead of her mom and Megan had fallen asleep. She woke to hear her mom crying, begging to the queen for mercy.

"You've been given more than enough time to take care of this, Dahlia. It's been months and nothing has changed. You've left me no choice in the matter. Unless you do as I ask."

"I cannot, my lady. I cannot do that to her. She is all I have."

Megan thought they were talking about her and had opened the curtain a little to see if her dad had been there as well. She saw him standing next to her mom sobbing.

"Then I have no choice but to strip your family of their magic and sentence you to the human world. I'm sorry, but that's all I can—"

"You can't expect me to live with the humans," Megan said. She remembered the look on the queen's face, thinking that she'd known she was there all along. "You think up something else. Whatever they've done isn't bad enough for you to make us go to the humans. I hate them."

"Whatever *they've* done? You're the one that has sentenced them to this, Megan. What did you expect to happen after you destroyed a part of the forest? Did you know that when you practiced your dark magic there, you killed over ten thousand plants? And because of that, nearly twice that in fairies and brownies are now without jobs?"

"So what? You're the queen, make it like it was before." Her mom had reached for her, and her dad had told her to hush. She'd snarled at him and told him to shut up, that he was useless to her. She was walking toward the queen to do what she couldn't remember now, but she wanted her to understand that she wasn't going to live in a world with humans, especially without magic.

One of the Royal Guard had stepped forward and blocked her. Megan could look back on it now and realize that confronting the queen on her own grounds had been stupid. Very much so. She should have waited until she was alone with her and tried to reason with her then. But the guard had stopped Megan from doing what she'd wanted and she'd lost control of her magic.

It was over in seconds. And in those few seconds, her father had been killed and her mother wounded. While Megan was being dragged away in chains, Lizzy had watched her humiliation. Then three days later, she and her mother and a nurse had been moved to the human world.

It had taken her mom a month to heal from the sword that had cut into her belly. She'd been cut badly while she'd been trying to save Megan's dad. But her mom had never healed from losing her mate. It was as if she'd been a ghost only moving through the motions of living and never speaking to her. Megan's mother never uttered a word to her from the day Megan's dad died until she joined him. On the day that Megan had turned nineteen and moved out, her mother went to her bed and never rose again. She'd died as quietly as she'd lived. And now this was going on.

~~~

Megan drove across town to where she knew the trash was picked up on Thursdays. She had to wait nearly ten minutes on one of the workers to get finished smoking before she could dump the body. But by then it was nearly dinner time and she was starving. Going through a drive-thru, she got a burger and fries and headed back. It was black as pitch in the alley, so she ate her quick dinner and then got out to get it over with.

The body was gone. Megan even drove out of the alley into the light to make sure, but the shower curtain and the body were gone. Panicky, she even looked under the truck to see if she was there and then in the dumpster. She was fucking gone.

Megan retraced her steps and realized that the only time she hadn't been with the truck and body was when she'd gone in to change. She thought about going door to door and asking her neighbors if they'd seen her, but she couldn't figure out how to ask. "Hey, I had a body in the back of my truck, did you take it?" seemed kind of stupid, and calling the cops because someone had stolen from her seemed equally stupid. She went to the basement and looked around, making sure that she'd not left the body there. She found nothing.

"Think, think, think. It has to be somewhere. Someone must have taken it and now they have…" She smiled as she thought of where the body might be. "Now they have to deal with her."

Megan went to her apartment and splurged on a bottle of wine and some ice cream. After she'd drank about half, she'd gone to bed feeling pretty good about herself. In the morning, she decided she was going to have a sale in celebration. And by evening, she should have Logan. Maybe she would give him back to Lizzy all beat to hell as a nice wedding gift.

~~~

Mel stood when Logan and Lizzy came toward her. She'd sent her guard for them the moment her man had returned to the castle. He'd called her, then the doctor, but it was too late to save her. Lula Burris was going to die.

"I can't use my magic on her because of the extensive damage done to her brain. Someone has…she's been hurt too badly for me to save even if I could."

Lizzy nodded, and Logan sat down.

"I didn't know we'd find her there, I swear it. I only used the mirror to see her and keep tabs on her. That's all, I swear it."

"Mel, sit down, please. You said she was dying. May I see her?" Logan asked.

Mel nodded and one of her men took him to the infirmary. She looked at Lizzy. "I'm so sorry I didn't step in sooner. I didn't know." Lizzy stood and went to sit beside her. She held her as she sobbed. That poor little boy had lost his mother because she'd been too late. When she was able to stop crying, she looked up at Lizzy.

"You said you used the mirror. I don't understand."

She nodded at the younger woman and smiled.

"Is it a magical mirror like the witch from those movies use?"

"No, it was a bottle, a green bottle. Remember how they worked? You would put it out where the one you were watching would touch it. Once they did, the bottle would act as a sort of GPS for the one who had cast it. I thought if she got close to any of you, I'd be able to warn you. But she didn't leave and I nearly stopped it. But then the bottle broke and her blood mixed with the magic and I was able to see her intent. And the woman."

"Lula Burris. What was she doing to her?"

Mel got up to pace the room, not really wanting to answer her.

"Mel?"

"She was dead then. Or as close as she could be. Nothing in the human world would have saved her and I thought by bringing her here she'd have a chance. For Mathew. But her mind had been scrambled. Megan had raped her mind harshly and made whatever magic I could have saved her body with null with her brain dead in so many places."

Logan came back and sat down. He looked like he didn't know what to do, and before she could apologize, he thanked her. She looked at Lizzy before looking back at him. "I don't understand. Or you don't. I could have saved her, but I didn't. Mathew is never going to forgive me for th—"

"Mathew will never know how she died or by who," he told her. "He'll know that you tried to save her and that you'd been watching over her, but I won't lie to him about what you think you didn't do."

He leaned forward and started to take her hands and stopped. Instead, she took his. She reached for Shamus and asked him to join them and to forgive Logan for what he was doing.

As he walked in the door, he leaned down and hugged Lizzy, a fair trade to touching her, she supposed he thought, then he sat with her on the couch and nodded to them both. "I'm sorry for your loss. I know that you two weren't on the best of terms, but losing someone hurts. And as many times as I've been to battle, it never gets any better." Logan nodded. "Mellie tell you what happened?"

"Yes, and I was just telling her that she did everything she could. Mathew will be grateful to know that she wasn't alone when she died, and that…" Logan stood up and then stopped. "I'd like to bring him here to see her, so he can say goodbye, but not…is there a way to make her less…abused?"

"Yes. We can do that." Mel nodded to a guard and had them go back for Mathew. "You'll need to tell me what to do before he gets here. I've asked Sara and Aaron to come with him. You've told him, told Mathew?"

"Yes. He's waiting for me to make sure it was her. He didn't say much, but I think he knows it's bad." Mel stood to go with Logan and let him continue while she made the woman look like he'd asked. "I always knew that she'd end up in the wrong hands. Hers mostly, but I knew that she'd pass early. She was wild and dangerous the entire time I knew her. Had it not been for her getting pregnant with Mathew, I don't think I would have stayed with her as long as I did."

Mathew was escorted into the room by Lizzy. Aaron and Sara were right behind him. He looked so pale and terrified that Mel found she wanted to run and hide. When her grandmother and mom came in the room as well, she was so grateful that she nearly sobbed. Her grandmother took his other hand and walked to the bed with him.

No one said anything for several minutes. Mel wasn't sure if they were waiting on Mathew or his dad, but her grandmother broke the silence by asking Mathew what he wanted to do with her when she passed completely over.

"I don't know. Bury her, I guess." He looked at her then back at her grandmother. "Isn't that what you do here?"

"No. We take them out and find a special place for them in the glen. Do you know what a glen is?" He nodded. "Smart boy. Well, we take them to the glen and find a nice spot we'd like to sit in when we come to visit them. The fairies help us out by planting a ring of flowers around the area, and once she's buried there, we are presented with the final flower. It will never die, and anytime you want to visit her, you just put it in the ground and an image of them appears. Not like she looks now, but one from your own memories."

"That would be nice."

Mel looked at her grandmother and nodded. She could do that for him.

"Mathew, Mel will take you out tomorrow and we'll look around. Then when you're ready, we can have the fairies start. It can be there for as long as you need it, and they'll care for it for you." Mel felt a hand brush against her and she looked down. It was Logan's.

"Thank you for this."

She nodded.

"You're an amazing woman, and I'll never forget what you've done here today."

Mel nodded and then mouthed her thanks to her grandmother. She waved her off as she continued speaking to Mathew. When he seemed to grow restless, Lizzy took him in the other room and sat with him. Mel stayed with Lula.

"Do you know who did this to her?"

Mel looked at Aaron when he'd asked.

"I'd very much like to help you bring her to justice if you're involved."

"I am. It's Megan. She had her held in a basement where my guard found her. She was taking her to be…" She looked at Logan who told her to continue. "She was taking her to a dumpster a few miles from where she has the shop I was telling you about. I was able to get some information from Lula. She felt horrible, but she'd told Megan of your fear of dark closed spaces. That was on her mind when she died in your world."

"When will you be bringing her in?"

Mel looked away from Aaron.

"You can't, can you? You have to follow some rules of engagement or something equally stupid."

"You know that I have to follow the rules here as much as you do in your own world. It fucking sucks, but that's the only way I can make this work. She killed a human, so in my eyes, my hands are tied. When she does something to someone that belongs to me, then I can step in." She wanted to stomp her foot in frustration. "What would you have me do, Aaron? Kill every human that murders one of their own? I can't do that anymore than you can."

Aaron took a deep breath and let it out slowly. The guards had entered the room with swords drawn the moment she'd raised her voice. But they knew better than to touch Aaron. He was powerful, but he was also her family. Even when he was mad, she knew he'd never harm her, but they didn't trust that. They would hurt him for her, but she knew as well as most of them that many of them would be hurt badly in the process.

"I'm going to have a talk with her then."

She shook her head.

"You can't talk to her, but I can."

"No, don't yet. If she knows that we are aware of her, she'll move on and we may never find her again. If she thinks that she's gotten away, she'll get cocky again and do something stupid. We both know that Megan isn't incredibly smart."

Aaron agreed, but he wasn't happy.

When Mathew came back, his eyes were red and swollen, as were Lizzy's. Mel knew that they'd talked, and she knew that Lizzy would be there for the little boy. At just after sunrise the next morning, Lula Barrett Burris passed away, never waking to see those around her. Mathew held her hand as she took her last breaths, and when she did, he went to his dad and new mom and let them hold him as he cried.

Chapter 11

Logan moved along the offices of his building without really seeing anything. He wasn't sad because Lula was gone, but he was in shock. He thought that Mathew was taking it much better than he was and smiled when he thought of why. Aaron and his family had been there with him the entire way. And Lizzy had been as protective as a bear when it came to him. He was sitting behind his desk when his phone rang.

"Mr. Burris, you will be here in the morning for the sale of the buildings downtown, will you not? There has been some…well, the city had an unexpected expense and if you back out now, we could be in trouble, major trouble."

Logan rubbed his forehead as the mayor spoke.

"The fire station just collapsed. Trucks and all were inside. No fire fighters, mind you, but the equipment was a loss. I just don't know what we'll do now. Not at all."

Logan had told them that the building was in bad shape, and at one point had offered to lend them the money to get it updated. But the city had very little money and less in the way of taxable income. He was reaching for a file when Aaron knocked on his door.

"I'll be there, Mr. Mayor. I have an appointment in the early morning I can't miss, but I'll be there at eleven as we'd discussed." The mayor thanked him several times and finally,

Logan had to hang up on him. "The fire house collapsed last night and now the city doesn't have any equipment."

"I know. I received a call earlier this morning asking if our department could help them out for a while. That's why I'm here. I wanted to talk to you about a few things."

Logan nodded and leaned back in his chair as Aaron got comfortable.

"What are your plans after this mess is over?"

"I plan to move into our new home and make love to my wife every chance I get. Why?" Aaron growled and Logan grinned. "If you didn't want me to tell you then you shouldn't have asked."

"I was thinking more along the lines of a job. What if I asked you to come and work for me? I can always use a good man in my corner."

Logan sat up, surprised.

"There's also the matter of the buildings you're set to purchase tomorrow. I'd like to go into partnership with you on them. I want to expand out so that more of my people will have a place to go if they are out when the sun rises."

"You mean like a safe house?"

Aaron nodded.

"There are actually nine buildings for sale. I only wanted two of them and the third was a part of the package. Your expansion, does it include those other buildings?"

"Yes. You remember Maddy? You met her when Dunc was born." Logan nodded. "She's the attorney I use when I need some buildings purchased. But this city councilman of yours, he won't talk to her because she's a female, and he's playing hardball with the others I've sent in as well. He knows, you see."

Knows? Before Logan could ask him what he meant, it occurred to him. "What is he? If he's a vampire, can't you just order him to do what you said?"

"If he was, but he's not. He's a bear. Bears are sort of pissy to begin with, and he's holding out because he thinks I've done something to him that requires me to apologize to him."

Logan laughed.

"I find that the thought of doing that goes against everything I am."

"Of course it does. And the great Aaron MacManus has standards. I think I know where Lizzy gets her stubbornness."

"Her mother." Aaron said it so quickly that Logan had a feeling he'd been telling people that for a long time. "But I would like to go into partnership with you."

"I'll have a lawyer draw something up."

Aaron called for Maddy, and a beautiful woman walked in.

"Are all the women you know drop-dead gorgeous or just the ones you have working for you?"

"All of them. And she's already drawn up the papers. It says that you and I split everything down the middle from costs to profits. And when one or either of us wants out, we sell for what we put in and nothing more."

Logan glanced over the document, then looked at Aaron. "This says that we'll be partners on all the buildings. I thought you said you only wanted the ones at the other end."

"I want a partner. You're my new son-in-law, and you should be a part of it." Aaron nodded to Maddy, who handed him the rest. "That's the deed to the house. I meant to give it to you yesterday, but forgot."

"Look, Aaron, this is great and all, but…well, I don't have the kind of money that it'll take to buy even half those buildings. I was struggling to get the three. And the insurance isn't coming through on this place or the house. We have no furniture yet and…" Logan smiled. "I'm broke."

"Not really." He looked at Maddy. "You're mated to a very wealthy woman. And as of this morning, you are wealthy as well."

"I don't want her money," Logan said and flushed when he realized how that had come out. "I mean, I'll provide for us. She doesn't have to dip into her money so that we can live day to day."

"Logan, do you know how old I am?"

Logan nodded at Aaron.

"Nearly two thousand years is a long time to save money, don't you think?"

"Yes, but—"

"But nothing. You forget that when we go into partnership together, I'm not talking for the next twenty years or even thirty. I'm talking lifetime. Our kind of lifetime. Centuries and centuries of lifetimes. You think in all that time you won't become as rich as me?"

"Christ, I'm immortal."

Aaron nodded.

"And...what about my son? I can't watch him...I never thought of this."

"Most don't. You'll be able to convert him if he wants when the time is right. But we're talking about us. Do you want to plan for your future or not?"

Logan nodded.

"Then sign the damned papers. I've got to get home before I explode."

Logan picked up his pen and signed the sheets where Maddy had put tabs. As soon as he had done the same for both copies, Aaron disappeared and Maddy grinned at him.

"There's more, isn't there?"

She nodded.

"Am I going to be pissed or am I going to be thrilled? I'm thinking pissed."

"Pissed. Hopefully not too pissed, but enough. You're not just a partner on the buildings that you sign off on tomorrow, but all of them. Including the ones in the Market District and the hospital and library that are being built for the same area. You're one fifth owner in all of those, but only half with the ones you're going to purchase with just Aaron."

"He tricked me."

She shook her head.

"Then what would you call it? We were talking about the buildings downtown and now I'm in partnership in a shit ton more."

"Yes, you are. As of the moment you put your name on those papers, you're now worth just over six billion dollars with cash, property, and investments. With the share of Lizzy's money, that makes you worth just over one hundred billion." She stood up and handed him a thick file. "Congratulations, Logan, you're a very wealthy man."

She was gone for perhaps an hour when he looked up. The file she'd given him was full of all the properties he now owned with men he barely knew. But each of them had sent a note with the file congratulating him on mating with Lizzy and welcoming him to the group. The group that had been called B.A.C.K. after Bradley Wolfe, Aaron MacManus, Colin Larimore, and Kyle Dixon was now called B.L.A.C.K. His name had been added to the names as well.

He called Lizzy and told her what had happened. She had been surprised a little, but not entirely. Her dad was a great man, she'd told him, and Logan told her he'd figured that out too.

"You're not so bad yourself, you know?" She laughed and he felt it all the way through the phone. "You think maybe we can go shopping for some things for the living room? I'm a little tired of sitting on lawn furniture. It was sort of fun the first night, but my ass is feeling it."

"I would love to. And something besides a mattress for Mathew's room. I think the adventure of camping out is over for him. Also, I was going to ask you about getting him a computer for his room. I think he'd be responsible with it. My grandda is helping him with his journal. Pete said she could hook us up."

He agreed with her and told her to have Pete set it up for him. Smiling, he thought he could afford a whole damned house of equipment like that if they wanted.

He told her he would meet her at the furniture store on Tenth, and he locked up his office and moved toward the door. He was pulling on his jacket when it hit him.

He was in love with her. Logan held onto the wall as what he'd just realized just rolled over him. He was deeply and completely in love with his mate. Smiling, he went to the parking garage and toward his car.

A scent he'd only smelled once before assaulted his nose, and he paused to turn. A flash of something moving past him had him reach for Lizzy as something hit him hard. But Aaron was all he could think of as he fell forward. Lizzy would come to him, but she'd have Mathew.

"Aaron, it's a wolf. Dirty, hurt, and he smells like Lula."

Darkness surrounded him as Aaron entered his mind and commanded him to look. Logan opened his eyes to see a license plate before he blacked out.

~~~

Mel was waiting for her when she entered the store. Mathew ran to her only to come up short as two men dressed in very nice suits stepped out in front of him. Lizzy felt her world come crashing down around her and if not for someone holding her up from behind, she would have fallen.

"I've got you." Her dad. "Come now, don't make a scene. People don't need to know that we've hit a bump in the road."

She nodded, knowing that he was trying to calm her, but she could feel his fear as well. She moved toward Mel as Mathew had, but she wasn't stopped. Mel was holding Mathew's hand and speaking to him softly.

"What's happened?" Lizzie asked.

Mel nodded to her as one man put his arm around her, the other around her dad. In seconds, they were in the antechamber of her castle. Lizzy asked her again what happened. But her dad spoke first.

"Someone took Logan. I have Pete looking for the car now." She looked at him to ask him where, but he held up his hand. "Let me tell you, Lizzy. I'm terrified beyond words now, just let me tell you."

She nodded and smiled at Mathew. "Draco is waiting for you. Do you remember where the pool is?" He nodded. "Good. He said that he has a gift for you. And something he and Tess are going to train you on. Are you going to learn to fight with a sword too?"

He nodded. "Lizzy, don't send me away. I know that something happened to my dad. I'm not a little kid right now, and as my dad says, there's enough tension in this room to make a murky soup. I know it's bad, but I also know that my dad is tough, tougher now because of what you gave him."

"Gave him?" She went down on her knees to look into his eyes. "Tristan. I see. He should have asked me or your dad before telling that. Do you know what will happen to him and to us if anyone finds out you have this information?"

"Tristan said that he'd be tied down and the sun would kill him. But I won't tell. Not ever." He wrapped his arms around her tightly and held her. "Mom, please don't let anyone hurt my dad."

Lizzy didn't know what was going on, but whatever it was, this little guy just made it all the more bearable. Hugging him to her, she told him she would do everything in her power to make sure that if he was hurt, the person would pay and pay dearly.

He nodded against her shoulder and held her a few more moments before he pulled back. Nodding again, he moved to the door, but stopped and turned to her before he left. "I know you'll help him. I love you, Mom."

Lizzy sat down hard on the floor. Her dad came to kneel down in front of her much as she'd done for Mathew. He was smiling at her. She let him help her up.

"Feels wonderful, doesn't it? To have someone acknowledge you like that?"

She nodded, unable to speak yet.

"The first time you said 'Dad,' I told everyone. Colin finally asked me to go away. He said I'd told him sixty-six times, and if I said it the sixty-seventh, he was going to murder me, master or not."

"Where is he, Dad?"

They both looked at Mel when she cleared her throat. She didn't look any happier than Lizzy did. But she also looked like a queen.

"I've two hundred of my best out looking for him. She must have him in a lined cell because I can't find him. I take it you've tired?"

Lizzy nodded and said, "When I didn't see his car in the lot, it was as if I was hitting a wall. I figured he was either in the elevator or he was blocking me. He does it without thinking right now. I think we'll have to work on that when he…"

"We'll get him back. I swear it."

She nodded to her dad.

"Logan was able to show me the license plate on the vehicle," he said. "It might be stolen, but it will give us a place to start. Your mom has gone to the building that Megan's shop is in. Logan also told me that he smelled wolf and Lula. Plus, he said 'dirty' and 'hurt.' I haven't been able to figure that one out."

"Bradley is looking too then?"

"Yes. I called him as soon as I talked to Logan. He said that he'd get out there right away before too many scents were mingled with that of the wolf." Her dad held her hand as he continued. "We'll find him love. I promise you."

"Tell him that by 'dirty,' Logan means sweaty. He calls someone who needs a bath 'dirty' and 'filthy' when they just stink. 'Hurt?' I'm assuming he smelled blood. He might not know the difference."

Pete was escorted in the room by two guards. They stayed back from her, Lizzy noticed. Finally, they were learning not to crowd her. She'd hurt a few of them when they had. She had her computer bag and a huge smile. She hugged Lizzy before she sat down.

"The plate doesn't belong to a blue anything. When your boy Logan looked at the plate, your dad said he saw blue. The car it's registered to is lemon yellow. The owner works at the mall, so I had a couple of pack members go out and have some fun. A shitty yellow two-door was sitting next to a nice Porsche. Don't that just suck?" Her dad said Pete's name and she stuck her tongue out at him. "Anyway, the idiots who stole the plate put theirs on it. How stupid do you need to be to be a bad guy? Apparently really stupid. The blue van they used to pick up Logan is registered to an Ollie Wright. He isn't from around here, and I've put out an all call on where he is. If he's here without permission, which I'm betting he is, Bradley will tear him up."

He would too. And then whoever was with him, and the pack they were from would pay dearly as well. Bradley was a great alpha and took care of his pack with a firm but fair hand. He handled things like this, where his rules were broken and people hurt, with a firmer hand, and there wasn't a drop of fairness in it. He'd kill the man and any that were with him. The pack they were from would pay a fine big enough to hurt badly too.

The van was found just after midnight, and Logan's blood was in the back. Not a great deal, but enough to make her know he'd been hurt. She watched as pack ran all over it, searching for anything when David, her longtime friend and brother to Bradley, came to where they were standing.

"I've found something." He handed her a small receipt. "It might not be anything, but I'm not taking any chances. It's dated for last night, and the time is before Logan contacted Aaron."

Pete came to her and Lizzy handed it to her. If anyone could figure it out, she would. Walking away, she promised Lizzy that she'd be back in a few minutes. She didn't even make it to her computer before she came back smiling.

"It's from Lou's out on seventy-nine. I stop in there all the time and get gas and a candy bar. I'd know this receipt anywhere." She showed it to Lizzy. "See here, they bought gas and four drinks. Logan was out, so that means there were four of them. Unless they were two and doubled up. I doubt it, but it could be. Gas was a fill up, I would imagine with that amount, or pretty close. So wherever he's been taken is far and not within a city."

David nodded and called for one of the men who'd come with him. "All that from a tiny scrap of paper."

Pete nodded. "And the one that handled this was a wolf and not from the Brotherhood either."

Men scattered after David spoke to them. Pete went to her computer, and Lizzy stared at the van. Logan had been in it and left them clues. She started to turn away with her dad when she turned to him suddenly. "Dad, I love him."

He smiled.

Holy shit, she was in love with her mate.

CHAPTER 12

Logan watched the door. He had no idea where he was, but it was cold and wet, with the scent of mildew in the air. He tried again to contact Aaron or anyone, and all he hit was a blank wall. When he shifted on his feet, something hard dug into his hip and he realized that he still had his phone. He was still trying to figure out how to get it out of his pocket with his hands tied when the door suddenly opened.

His sight was a little blurry, but he could see better now than he had been able to. The first time he'd awakened, he couldn't see anything and he hurt everywhere. He thought that Lizzy's blood was helping him. He didn't speak as the woman came toward him.

"He wakes." She walked around him and looked him over. "Lizzy always did have good taste. Even as a kid she had the best clothes, and her hair always looked like she'd stepped from a beauty parlor. I guess that didn't change once she got to picking men too."

She kicked him in the back before coming around to face him again. She knelt before him and smiled. He wanted to grab her around the throat and choke the living shit out of her, but he just let her look.

"You smell like her and vampire. I'm guessing that she became one after she hit the right age. Can you tell me if she has a great deal of magic still, or did she lose that with her change?"

He didn't answer, but something rubbed against his mind. It wasn't like Lizzy had done, or even how Aaron had felt like when they'd been practicing, but like he'd thought of someone rubbing against his mind to touch it, and not gently either.

The woman frowned at him. "She has your mind blocked. I guess I'll have to give her credit for that one. I can't hurt what I can't get into." She snapped her fingers, and a chair was brought in for her. "You have something of mine. Or that I want. The building that I have my shop in. You outbid me and now they're going to have to start the bidding all over. It's really too bad that you're not going to be there when it happens then either."

Logan watched her primp. His ex-wife had done that as well. It would get to the point that he would have to leave the room or scream at her to stop. He could never figure out what the fuck the reasoning behind straightening your shirt over your lap for ten to twenty minutes had to do with going to the store. She had to have everything just right. And when no one noticed her, she'd pout for hours afterward.

"Who are you?" He knew that when someone asked Lula that, she'd get pissy. He hated to think of his now deceased ex-wife like that, but he was desperate to be released.

As if on cue, she kicked him in the shin. "You've never heard of me?" He didn't move. "Never? Even hanging around Lizzy, she never mentioned how I used to terrorize her as a child?"

Logan pretended to think about it. Then shook his head and smiled. "Wait. You're that girl that she knocked on her ass with a punch to the face? Oh yeah, she told me about that. We had a good laugh. Colin is teaching my son the—"

His head hit the wall behind him twice before she sat back in her chair. Her fist had come out quickly and had jabbed him hard twice in the jaw. When he turned back to her, he had to keep his mouth closed because his fangs had dropped. Logan didn't know why he thought so, but he had a feeling that Megan didn't know he was a vampire like his Lizzy was.

"She cheated. She used magic back on me when I was told no more. Then that fucking cunt of a queen stepped in and made me stop coming to the classes. She said she can tell when someone uses magic, but she lied to get her precious Lizzy to continue. I could have been great. I will be great when you're gone."

He watched her as she ranted on and on then when she noticed him again, she seemed to try and calm herself. But her true self had come through.

"Tomorrow, I'm going to call your wife and tell her that if she wants you back, she'll give me money. A lot of it too. She's going to pay for getting me kicked out of the kingdom. The queen will know that I've succeeded, and things will get much better for me and my store." She looked behind her when a man came into the room. "What the fuck do you want?"

"We was wanting to know if we can go out now that you're here? My guys are hungry and they are snapping at each other. And we gotta report to our alpha."

She snarled as she stood up.

"You have to let them eat or things'll go bad for us all."

"Go then. But if anything happens, I'm holding you responsible. Those idiots out there are going to get us caught, and I'm not going to jail for their stupidity."

The man growled. Even Logan could tell he was warning her. But she only shoved him out of the cell and locked the door behind her. Logan leaned his head back against the wall and tried to reach someone again.

When this was over, he decided he was going to learn all he could about what he could do and what he was. Closing his eyes, he tried to think of some of the things that Lizzy had shown him, but other than biting and talking to her, there wasn't much else.

Morrigan, the witch. She owed him. He wasn't sure if this would be considered part of the two more questions or not, but he was willing to try. Closing his eyes, he thought of her. Then he called her name in his mind. Nothing. He opened his eyes to see her sitting before him. Logan grinned.

"You're a very intelligent man. Do you know that most men just call me because they want a favor? You don't, do you?"

He shook his head.

"You do know that I can't change the outcome of this. I'm not one of the Fates, but only a witch. Powerful, yes, but still only a witch."

"More than a witch, I think, and you well know it. I know how some of this thing works, and probably just enough of that to get me into hot water. You said I had two questions I could ask." He started to ask her if that was correct, but was afraid she'd count it against him. When she laughed, he decided he had to be crafty with her.

"I will enjoy this, I think. And yes, you have two questions. But I will give you something first. I cannot tell them where you are. I cannot tell them how you are as well. If your question is for me to ask one of them, then you will waste it. I am not able to interfere with the ways things are set into motion."

Logan nodded. He had to do this right or he wouldn't be able to get out of this. He looked at the woman. She was going to help him, but...

"I have a phone in my pocket. I need for you to take my picture." She looked at him for several seconds. "Or can't you do that?" He was playing with fire and knew it. She was a witch, not an idiot, and he was hoping that she'd see that he was trying to get back to his family.

124

"I can take your picture. I can even send it to someone for you. Not a question, I get that, but don't push your luck."

He felt his phone leave his pocket. She hadn't moved, but suddenly, his camera was in the palm of her hand.

He tried to think what to do. He thought about smiling to show he was fine, but that wouldn't work. Then he realized she was smiling at him. It wasn't a friendly smile, and all he could think about was he hoped it wasn't directed at him.

"It's not. I'm taking this picture now." The camera clicked, then she held it up seemingly to inspect it. "But I'm not sure just how to send it. How about if I take it to Lizzy? Or Aaron? One of them should be able to see that you're well enough in it, don't you think?"

"You would know best."

She stared at him for a long while. Then she leaned back. She seemed to be in no hurry, and as much as he wanted her to go and find his family, pissing her off wouldn't help.

"When Lizzy was born, and so you know, it's important that you know her entire name is Melody Savannah Elizabeth MacManus. It was determined that she would be the catalyst to all vampires to be brought together. Her brother would be as well, but Lizzy and her mate were to be greatness."

"And now she's not? If I had anything to do with you changing your mind, I'm sorry. But I won't lose her. I just figured out that I love her."

She smiled at him.

"Morrigan, are they going to be all right?"

It was one of his questions, but he didn't care. He needed to know. He wouldn't give up if she told him they wouldn't; he'd just try harder to get to them. She stood and looked to the door. He knew someone was coming and braced himself for their return.

"Don't let them win, Logan. You're much smarter than them. Just keep your secrets safe and you'll be fine. I'll be back if you need me. But I doubt you will." Then she was gone and the door opened and three large men and Megan came in.

"I need a bit of your blood so I can show them that I have you." Megan said with a smile. "I guess I could just ask you for it, but this way is so much more fun."

The bullet ripped into his shoulder and he cried out in pain. The man who shot him looked pleased with himself, and Logan decided that as soon as this was over, he was going to tear the man apart.

~~~

"Lady Lizzy, there is a person here to see you. She is the witch Morrigan. She said that it is important that she has a word with you." Duncan didn't look, happy and Lizzy asked him what had happened. "She is not here, my lady. She is here but not here. If you know what I mean."

She didn't, but went into the living room to speak with her. Morrigan looked like she always did. Black clothing and dark hair. She was so beautiful. Lizzy had always thought so. But Duncan was right; she wasn't here, just her image.

"I have something for you. Your mate is a very smart man. I want to strangle him, but he is a smart man." The phone appeared on the table between them. "He asked me to take his picture. I'm not sure if I did a good job or not, so I practiced a bit more taking pictures of other things. I think I did well when I compare them all together."

Lizzy picked up the phone and realized the battery was dead. She went to find a charger, and Morrigan followed her into the kitchen where her mom and Mel were. Morrigan smiled at them before sitting down on whatever it was at her end.

"She took a picture of Logan because he asked her to. Now the battery is dead." She plugged it in and looked at Mel. "I don't suppose you could charge it up now, could you?"

"I wouldn't do that."

Lizzy turned to Morrigan when she spoke.

"You know that we can't, Lizzy. Taking the picture was almost bordering on helping with the outcome. The Fates are nasty when they're—"

"Fuck the Fates." Lizzy sat down and started to cry. "I need him, don't you understand? I need him and I love him. I want him here, not with that mad woman. I can't help him if he's where I can't find him."

"But you can."

Lizzy stood up when Atropos, Clotho, and Lachesis, the Sisters Three, or the Fates, shimmered into the room. Clotho smiled at Morrigan, but said nothing more.

"What do you mean I can? I can what? Find him? In case you haven't been paying attention, I have been trying to find him. She has him in some sort of lined cell and I can't break through that."

"No, you can't," Atropos said. "Morrigan, how did you find our young Logan? Was he well when you left him? I have heard that he was shot just after you left. I have checked since and he seems to be holding up well."

Lizzy would gladly have shot them all if she thought it would do any good. But they'd just turn her into something and leave her that way forever. She looked at Mel. "How do you do this every day? I mean, how do you put up with beings that you'd like to murder?"

Mel laughed as she answered her. "You should listen more and talk less, Lizzy. They are giving you a way."

Lizzy turned to the women and frowned.

"Listen."

Atropos winked at Mel, then turned to Morrigan. "Anyway. Logan. Did you know that he's the one we picked for our Lizzy all those decades ago? And now he's there and without knowing if he's going to make it."

"He's going to make it. I'll kick his ass if he even thinks that." Lizzy looked at Morrigan then Mel. "You've seen him.

You've both been to see him. Including you." Lizzy pointed to the Fates, waiting for whatever was just out of her reach to click into place. Something that she'd missed. Mathew walked in and asked if he could have a sandwich, and she stood up to make him one.

"I've been helping Tristan. He said that with my help on the virtual imaging, he might be able to retool the game so that he could re-release it."

Lizzy handed him the plate with the sandwich on it and froze.

"Can you let it go, Mom?"

"Virtual imaging." She looked at Morrigan when Mathew left the room with his sandwich and then threw her arms around her. "I can see him. I can...Oh my God, I can see him. How do I do...never mind. I'll figure it out." She went to find her grandfather. He'd help her and be excited about it. She found him in the study playing with a computer with Pete.

He looked up at her with a smile. "Come here, my dear. You must see your son's pictures and captions. He is quite clever. And he has a steady hand when he uses the camera we gave him as well."

She walked to the computer and was shocked.

"Well done, aren't they?"

"Yes, they are." He flipped through a few of them and she could see that he was having fun at it too. When he got to the end of them, she stood up and thanked Pete.

"Don't thank me, thank him." She pointed at her grandfather. "This was his idea to keep him busy. Between us and Tristan, the kid is bouncing around us like he's running a flipping war room. I'd hate to work for him."

She laughed and turned to her grandfather. "I need your help too. I need to go to Logan and speak to him, but I'm not sure how to do it. The way you and Grandmother can appear in a room without being here."

"Oh that's easy. You just have to dream." He laughed when she raised a brow at him. He pressed his finger over it. "You got that from your father. I've never met a man who could say so much with a brow before. He can—"

Pete cleared her throat. Lizzy laughed. Her grandparents could go on about nothing at all more than anyone she knew. He moved to the couch with her and took her hand.

"It's really very simple. At first, you'll fade in and out, but he'll just be glad to see you and he won't notice. You'll, of course, need to peek in the room before going in. If he's with another supernatural that you don't want to see, it will be all over."

She nodded. "And how do I do that?" His laughter made her smile. "Thank you, Grandfather. I love him so very much and I just want to talk to him."

He patted her leg. "Of course you do. Now, here's what you do. It's the same principle as the link you have to speak to him. You send him images of you, correct?"

She flushed, but he didn't seem to notice. Pete did and burst out laughing. Lizzy decided that she was going to get back at the woman if she had to wait ten decades to do so. Smiling, she turned back to her grandfather.

"Think of yourself as he'd see you. Sort of like you see in the mirror. Then you simply project yourself there, not your voice, but you. He doesn't really see you in his mind when you speak, but when you do this, everyone can see you that has the ability. Understand?"

She thought so and thought about him then stopped when her grandfather touched her hand.

"Peek first, love. Megan may be stupid, but she can see you if you let her. Peek by the way your father does when he wants to see what you're looking at. Through his eyes."

Through his eyes sounded easy enough, but she wasn't sure what to do. Leaving the study, she went to find her dad. This was turning into being something of a wild goose chase, but she had to try. Finding him in his office, she had to wait for him to get off the phone before she could ask for help.

"That was Bradley. And if you'd like to know what a pissed off alpha sounds like, call him back. Better yet, invite him over." Her dad smiled. "Actually, don't. I just had the carpets replaced and he may want to mark them. He just spoke to the other alpha. He is not a happy camper either."

"What's going to happen with the wolves?" Lizzy said and sat down. Her dad came to sit next to her. "Is the other alpha going to pay the fine for what his pack did to Bradley?"

"No. Poor bastard said that Bradley could have his pack. He told him that he was retiring anyway and his son was a moron. He basically told Bradley that if he wanted them to take them, and if some of them died in the process, he was happy with that too. He's called the Council in to oversee matters." He leaned back into the seat. "Tell me what I can do to help. And just so you know, I like this young man a great deal."

"I do too. In fact, I love him very much. I want to see him, but I don't know how. Grandfather told me how to do it, but I have to peek into the room first so that Megan, if she's there, can't see me."

He smiled. "Brilliant plan. I should have thought of it myself. Smart girl of mine, you are."

She started to tell him that Morrigan had helped, along with the Fates, but didn't. Her dad and the ladies didn't see eye to eye on the whole magic thing. The ladies told him it was magic that he used, and he said it was skill. Whatever it was, she needed a bit of whatever all of them had.

Chapter 13

Logan felt the connection to Lizzy, but before he could pounce on it and speak to her, she was gone. The pain he felt over that loss was great and he wanted to scream out in frustration. Then he felt something, a kind of stir in the air, and suddenly, she was there.

"Don't talk until I can figure out what I'm doing."

He grinned at her tone. She sounded like Mathew when he couldn't get a math problem to work out. She faded out some, but not completely.

"Okay, Dad said to tell you that I'm backwards. I don't know why that's important, but he said that I'm not very good at this, which I've pointed out to him several times. I'm here, aren't I? But when I was told to think of…forget it. It's not important. I love you."

"I love you too. Oh, love, I love you so much." He watched her fade again. Then he noticed she was looking to her right, or left, he didn't really care, but he knew that she was talking to someone. "Lizzy? What's going on?"

"I got your picture. Are you hurt? They said you'd been shot."

He nodded to his shoulder that was all but healed.

"Dad had asked for proof of them having you and we just received a cloth with your blood on it. She shot you?"

"One of her henchmen did. Is Mathew all right?"

She nodded and wiped at tears.

"Don't cry, love, please. Get me home and I'll hold you forever."

"I need for you to help us find you. Are there any sounds where you are? Bradley said to raise your nose to the air and open your mouth and breathe in. It's a trick so we can absorb more of what's around us."

Logan did as she asked. He wasn't sure what he was trying to pull in and was having a little trouble separating the tastes to try and figure out what they were. He tried breaking them down one at a time like he did business contracts.

"Wolf, of course, and burnt something…wood, I guess." He did it again. "No, not wood but coal. I can smell coal. And flowers. I can smell roses and daisies and marigolds. I can smell herbs like basil and thyme. There's oregano too, strong and sharp. Lizzy, it smells like a greenhouse."

"That helps." She turned to someone again, and he figured it was Pete. "Now sounds. I've taken the liberty of sort of turning down your volume, I guess. Making it so that you can hear, but not as I do or any other supe does. What can you hear? And remember that you can hear like a wolf. Things that you normally wouldn't hear are going to be painful."

He felt the moment she stopped turning it down. Things weren't just painful, but overwhelming. He looked at her when she stood up. She was pacing and talking.

"Dad said for you to focus on the sharp ones and turn them down one at a time. I'm sorry, Logan, I wish I could have helped you more." He smiled at her and told her he loved her. "I love you too and plan on showing you, but we have to focus here. Get to listening."

He could hear everything, painfully so. Some of them were so loud that, like she'd said, they hurt. But then he realized that they weren't really loud at all but higher pitched. Those were the ones he tried to sort out. One by one he went through them, pushing them to the back of his mind and putting the others in a sort of box to think about later.

"I can hear cars. Not a lot, but two maybe, three going by me. Water. Somewhere there's water splashing against something…metal maybe?" As he listened, he heard something else, something curious. "I hear children. They're talking about a test. Something about a state test that…Christ, there's a school nearby."

"Good. Water and a school. Pete is looking. What else? You're doing fantastic."

He smiled and closed his eyes this time. It was getting easier, but no less frustrating. His eyes popped open. "Someone just paged for Denton that he has a phone call on line six. And she said there was a sales meeting at nine."

She turned away and he heard them coming and told her.

"I'll be back. I love you, so you stay strong."

The door opened just as she disappeared. He dropped his head down so they couldn't see the smile that he was sure was going from ear to ear. He'd helped her find him, he knew. When Megan kicked out at him, he looked up at her.

"It's about ten minutes from when your deal is going to go bust. I just wanted to be here to watch your face when you realize that I won."

He didn't say a word. What would be the point?

"The big and bad Logan Burris lost to a halfling."

"Halfling?"

She flushed probably not realizing until then what she'd said. But he'd heard her.

"Yes. My mother was a fae and my father human. They loved each other so much that they didn't care that when they had me I'd be nothing more than a halfling. But I showed them. I showed them all, and now I'm going to take something that they all love."

"Lizzy."

~~~

"Are you ready?"

Lizzy looked at Maddy and tried to think about what she was saying to her.

"Lizzy, if you're not going to do this, just say so. I can take this old bastard on if I have to."

"No. I was thinking about something else. He said children and a page about a phone call. I don't think it's a school." She shook her head. "I'm ready. Let's do this."

Elijah Peterson was on the city council of their town. Actually, he was the entire council. No one else had wanted the job and now that the city was having so many financial problems they could only afford him. He wasn't a particularly nice man, and Lizzy figured that, as a bear, he probably wasn't nice then either. And he hated her dad. She smiled at the memory.

Her mom and dad had been out. Lizzy hadn't ever figured out what they had been doing, and after all this time, had never had the inclination to ask. She was pretty sure, but like most kids, didn't want to think about it. But at some point, they'd crossed paths with Elijah.

He'd been fishing in the great pond on her parents' property. Not with a pole, but as a bear, and he'd been showing his son, another Elijah, how to catch them with his claws and toss them up on the shore. While her parents had been watching this, apparently one of the fish had hit her mom.

No one but Elijah the senior had been upset. Her mom had told her she thought it was funny. They had been watching, but it had been their fish and pond. Elijah had come running after them, out of the water in great leaps until he was nearly on top of them. Her dad had simply protected his mate. He'd punched Elijah in the nose. But that hadn't been what had brought on the hatred.

Elijah the child had laughed. Great, loud resounding peals of laughter that had brought out other animals to see what was going on. Elijah senior, nose bloodied and embarrassed, had risen up on his hind legs and roared at his son. The boy only laughed harder until in his anger, he'd run after the boy and had slapped him.

His claws had raked across the boy's face and tore it open, harshly. As Elijah had stood there looking pole-axed, her dad had pulled the boy from the water and immediately tore open his wrist to save him. Within minutes, seconds really, her mom told her that the wounds had sealed and the boy had nothing more than bloody fur to show for what had happened. Except for his mistrust now for his dad. And that was why whenever he could, Elijah would go out of his way to thwart her father on anything and everything because he'd always felt that Aaron had thought to save his son and not him. Stupid Lizzy always thought the man should have been grateful but he had lost face with the others who had witnessed him hurting his son.

Logan's name was called, and Lizzy stood up and straightened her suit. Taking a deep breath, she moved forward. When she smiled at Sam Luna, the bailiff, he nodded and winked. He was a wolf in Bradley's pack and she'd known him all her life.

"It says here that Logan Burris is supposed to be here to put in his bid. You're not Logan."

She shook her head and handed Sam what she had to prove that she could come here and represent her husband.

"You any relation to that Aaron MacManus?"

"He's my dad."

Elijah tossed the papers onto the desk and glared at her. She waited for him to speak. For one, she was a great deal older than him, and two, she was more powerful even if he shifted to bear.

"I have other offers and I'll take his into consideration. As soon as I get them all, I'll—"

She cut him off. "No, you won't. You've seen the name MacManus and you figure you'll just stop this bid because you think my dad embarrassed you when you should be happy he saved your son. Well, I'm not going to sit here and wait for my town to go bust because you're an arrogant asshole who doesn't know when to say enough."

"Now see here. You can't talk to me that way in my—"

"In my courtroom, you overbearing, mean-minded prick?" Lizzy forgot she was supposed to be sweet and try to woo the council her way. She stretched her neck and took a deep breath. Fuck it, she was too stressed and too much like her dad to simply woo anyone. "There are nine buildings on that end of town that are sitting for the most part empty. No rent, no taxes, and no revenue. Why? I'll tell you why; there is no money. You have a fire department that can't make calls. Again, because of no money. You sit up there on your throne and turn down millions of dollars to someone who can help because you feel you've been slighted somehow. Well, grow the fuck up." She heard the door open behind her, but didn't turn. "I propose that you pick up that fucking pen, sign the form, and let us buy the buildings. And in addition to that, we'll—my family and I—will lend the city the money to upgrade and revamp the fire station and the hospital."

"You'll no doubt want the MacManus name all over this too. The big, bad vamp rushes in to save the day again. Well, it won't happen. Not so long as I'm breathing, it won't."

She glared at the bear, lost her temper completely, and rushed to his dais. She picked him up by his throat. "That can be arranged, you stupid son of a bitch."

"Mrs. Burris…Lizzy, put my dad down."

She turned slowly to see the man who stood not five feet from her.

"Please, just put him down. Don't hurt him."

136

She wanted to drop him, but set him down gently. Elijah rubbed at the bruise already forming on his throat, and she felt horrible at what she'd done. She looked around the courtroom and was glad that only a few had seen her lose her temper and that all of them were like her and Elijah, supes. She jumped down to the floor and sat in one of the chairs that had been set up.

"Dad, what are you doing?" Elijah junior sat on the corner of the dais and looked at her before looking back at his dad. "You said to me just the other day that this influx of money would go a long way to help getting the town out of the red. Selling the other buildings you said would be easier if those sold. Now she comes in here wanting to buy them all and lend the city money, and you do this? Why?"

"Of course you'd side with the great MacManus. The man who would provoke me to hurt you and then had the nerve to save you." Elijah senior flushed. "That's not what I meant."

"Yes, it is. It's always what you mean. I was eight years old and thought the world of you. But you hit me, clawed me open, then just stood over me while he saved me. Not you, him. Then you kept on clawing me open every time you looked at me with that look. The one that says you hate me."

"I never hated you. I wasn't able to save you like he had. And he had no right. None at all to give you vampire blood."

Junior stood and shook his head.

"I have every right to hate the man."

"And I have every right not to." Junior started for the doors in the back of the room, but turned and looked back at his dad. "I have a son now, not that you'd know because I don't come around because of you. He's ten now and loves to go fishing with me. He loves me despite the fact that I have vampire blood in my veins. I think he's grateful to have it there. Without it, I would never have lived to have him."

He walked out and Lizzy turned away. Her heart broke for the man. Not the one who had just walked out, but the man at the dais. He looked broken, and she hurt for him.

"I can't..." He looked around the room and then back at her. "What have I done? Please, you have to help me."

She wanted to tell him to grow some balls and go after his son, but she needed this deal finished. She tossed the file in front of him and pulled as much of her mom as she could summon from herself. "You need this money; the city needs this money. The loan could save countless lives and bring back some much needed taxes, not just from this, but from more people moving back. No one wants to live in a town where there isn't a firehouse. And at the rate things are going, you won't have a police station either in a few more months." She picked up his pen and handed it to him. "Sign it, Elijah."

He nodded and took the pen. As soon as his signature was across it, she handed him the second one and asked Sam to bring in Maddy. This was the loan and the payment schedule she and Maddy had come up with.

It took twenty more minutes for him to go over it. He was pleased with it, and told her that he'd give it to the mayor if he hadn't left yet. She asked him where he was going.

"He gave his notice yesterday." He looked at her and smiled. "And I know just the man for the job. You think that husband of yours will take the spot until we can find someone to put on the ballot? Might go a long way for doing some of these improvements you have jumping around in that pretty little head of yours."

"I'll ask him. In the meantime, go and find your son. He's at the pack house with his wife and son. They've been there since Monday. It's an annual visit that we all look forward to. My dad will be there as well. Wouldn't hurt you to say you're sorry and tell him how grateful you are for him helping out."

138

"Your dad is helping me out? How the hell…" He seemed to forget he was supposed to be trying to make things work out not yell at her. "How is your dad helping me out?"

"He just bought the buildings and lent you money along with his partner, my husband." She waited for the explosion. When it came, she was shocked. He wasn't pissed like she thought he'd be, but his laughter was hearty and loud. She stared at him, thinking this was the first time in all the time she'd known him that she'd seen anything but a scowl on his face. This suited him much better.

"Lizzy?"

She turned back just as she and Maddy were leaving.

"Did your father put you up to this? And you should know that you're a great deal like him. Spitting image, if you want to know the truth."

She smiled. "Thanks, and sort of. He knew I was coming here, but he wasn't sure I'd be able to pull it off. He seems to think you're a hard-assed bastard too."

He laughed again. "Tell your husband that he has my vote, or yours for that matter. You ever think of going into politics, Lizzy?"

"No thanks. I have too much power as it is. Can't think what I'd do if you gave me any more. But I'll tell Logan. As soon as I get him back."

She was out the door before he could ask her to explain. Maddy stopped her halfway to the door. She was smiling. "You know he's right about you; you are your father's daughter. I thought I'd shit myself when you leapt up on his throne and picked him up. Sam is the only thing that kept me from doing it."

Lizzy nodded embarrassed.

"Lizzy, what you did in there is more than save this town. You know that, don't you."

"I don't really care right now. I want my mate back." She moved out of the building and into the street. Maddy had paperwork to file. She moved to her car and reached for Logan like she did almost every waking moment. Still nothing. Fighting tears until she was alone, she thought of what she was going to do to Megan when she found her.

CHAPTER 14

Logan heard the commotion before he saw anything. He'd been dozing and trying to think of anything but how much he wanted to get out of here. Moving his legs slightly, he looked at the door and held up his hand. He'd been playing with his magic all night and had a surprise for whoever came through the door.

A wolf tore the door off its hinges and Logan was ready to blast him when Bradley was suddenly there. Logan barely had enough time to move the spray of magic away before the man jumped back out of the way. When he started cussing on the other side of the door, Logan smiled.

"You have a very colorful way of stringing words together there, alpha. Does your mate know what you do with that mouth of yours when she's not around?"

He came into the room with a large gray wolf and smiled. "She's very pleased with what I do with my mouth, thanks. But you scared the shit out of me. Lizzy said you had very little skills in the magic department."

"I was playing around and figured it out. Not really very good at it yet, but it might have taken out a guard or two."

Bradley nodded.

"I don't suppose she's with you, is she?"

"Yes. But I asked her to find Megan. I doubt she will, but we'll find her soon enough. She's been gone long enough that

I can smell her, but nothing is fresh. I told her that she'd be better off finding the bitch, not my kind but general female kind, in the event that she circled around behind us and took us out."

He leaned over and tore the chains from the wall. Logan's arms dropped. They'd been tied up for so long that they burned now. His legs were unchained next.

"That power you have, why didn't you use it on your chains to free yourself?"

Logan lifted his pant leg and showed him the burn on his sock and shoe.

"Ah. Lots of power, but no control. It'll come to you sooner or later."

"In the meantime, I'm going to be without hair on my legs if I keep this up." He smelled her before she came around the corner. Lizzy, his Lizzy, was coming to him. Just as he managed to stand, she came around the doorjamb and into his arms. Nothing had ever felt so good.

"We found you." She kissed him on the face then pulled back. "Christ, you need a bath. What have you been doing, rolling in manure?"

"Yes, love, I have." He pulled her close to him again. "Not yet. I'm not ready to let go just yet."

The pack moved over the building he was in. When Logan went out of it and into the sunshine, he took several moments just to feel it on his skin. Aaron touched his mind as he stood there.

"I wish I could be there with you, but it's much too bright out and I need to rest. Are you well?" He told him he was. *"You come home and I'll give you a proper welcoming. There are some matters we must discuss, but I'll let you have a homecoming with your mate. My grandson has decided that he'd love to stay the night so that the two of you may watch television or whatever you want in my house, under my roof."*

Logan laughed at Aaron's none-too-veiled attempt to tell him no sex. *"He has, has he? Does it have anything to do with the fact that you're spoiling him rotten? Or that you've given him everything he's asked for?"* Logan smiled. *"Or is it because you love him already?"*

"All the above, but mostly the last. And as for giving him everything, he asks for very little. The computer he has was a gift from Phillip because the two of them are working on a project together, and the game system was here already. Not being used much any longer, but I think that will change once you and Lizzy start having more children."

Children. He'd thought of it while he'd been chained up and wondered how that worked. He knew it was possible, of course, but not how often or how many they could have. Aaron laughed as he answered his unspoken question.

"As many as you wish, but in moderation, I would guess. Lizzy is human too, so I would guess that she could be pregnant. If you were having sex, that is. You're not having sex with my baby girl, are you, Logan?"

Logan grinned and actually thought about telling him no, but he was feeling much too good and told him the truth. *"If I can manage it, I'm going to have sex with her in the back of the limo that you sent for us to come home in."*

Logan looked around. There was a street nearby and he could see a greenhouse, Pedals and Roots, just across the street. It was small and out of place on the nearly empty street, but he decided that if he couldn't convince his new partner to help them along, he'd simply do it himself. He heard the small children behind him and turned.

"It's an orphanage."

He looked at Lizzy who was helping him into the car. He was still a little on the weak side. "It looks really run down." The playground equipment looked like it had been through a war zone with most of the swings missing or the chains broken. The slide had a chain across the ladder, but it didn't seem to stop the children from climbing over it and down the slope that shook with each ride. The building itself was falling in places with windows boarded up and graffiti on them as well as the brick. A couple, probably the ones who ran the place, were hanging sheets on the line, most of those worn through in places so badly that he could see their faces on the other side. He looked at her as she sat next to him.

"I've already taken care of things to have them moved to somewhere safer. We've purchased a building that can be renovated in less time than we could build. The one that you were held in, as a matter of fact. I was able to get Bradley and his construction crew to come out and start on it as soon as tomorrow."

He kissed her and pulled her onto his lap so that she was facing him. "You've been busy. What else have you done? I don't suppose we have a bed yet, do we?"

"Yes." She curled her fingers into his hair as he pulled her nipple through her shirt and bra into his mouth and nipped. "I've been shopping with my mom when I got to the point where I was ready to murder someone. Logan, you're going to have to stop this. We won't make it home, and I have such plans for you."

He rolled her to her back and settled between her legs. "I have some for you as well, but right now I need to be inside of you. Deep and hard."

Logan nuzzled her throat and licked along the pounding pulse. She moved her head and offered herself to him, but he wanted more, so much more. Lifting his body from hers slightly, he told her to feed him her nipple. She moved to unbutton her blouse, fumbling more than she was getting them undone. Frustrated, she tore it open and then unclasped her bra for him. He took as much of her breast into his mouth as he could and suckled.

"Logan, Christ." She rolled her hips up, and he rocked down into her. They danced like this, teasing each other, until he was ready to explode over her. Lifting his head from her breast, now bruised and red, he licked a path from there to her navel, biting her gently and not so gently as he went. Pausing at her waist, he ran his tongue around and around her small belly button and moaned when her scent overwhelmed him.

He moved to the floor of the car and helped her pull her jeans off. She was soaked through the crotch of her pants, wet with her need. When they were off and tossed to the floor beside him, he ran his hands up her thighs and back down, watching her face while she moaned over and over.

"I want to drink from you."

She nodded and rolled her hips again.

"Will you come for me, Lizzy? Come in my mouth so I can gorge myself on you?"

"Please, Logan. I want to come in your mouth, but I need you inside of me too." She lifted her hips up as she braced her feet on his shoulders. "Fuck me, please."

He opened her wider with his fingers, spread her wide enough that she held no secrets from him. He suckled her clit into his mouth and moaned as paradise filled him. Moving his tongue into her sheath, she cried out for more.

He wasn't going to disappoint her.

Sliding his tongue in and out of her, he pressed his fingers into her as well, joining his mouth and filling her. Her juices poured from her and he drank greedily. Looking up at her face, he felt his heart skip several beats as he watched her.

Her breasts filled her hands as she cupped them, her nipples, red from his own mouth, were hard peaks where she was pinching and twisting them. Her head thrown back in primal repose looked beautiful, pure enjoyment written across her face as if the word had been invented just for her in this position. Watching her was amazing, and he fell more deeply in love with her.

"Come for me, Lizzy. Come so that I have as much enjoyment drinking from you as you're having." Putting his mouth over her clit, he slid his finger deep. Using his free hand, he moved up the crack of her ass, soaked with her copious hot cream, and pressed against her anus. She moaned loudly. When he slid into the tight muscles, she came apart, flooding his mouth and filling him.

Lapping quickly, he drank from her, feeling the same utopia as he did when he had bitten her. Thinking about that feeling, he felt his fangs drop. Need ripped along his skin as he thought about biting her, marking her. Logan was going to come; pressure built and his spine tingled with anticipation. Lifting his head, he ripped his pants open and freed his cock almost at the same time. Pulling her forward, he impaled her over him. Her legs wrapped tightly around him, he lifted her up and down and fucked her as he nuzzled her throat. When she bared her neck for him, his fangs burst with need and he bit her hard.

Blood, her blood, exploded in his mouth. As she came around him, milking his cock within her tight sheath, he drank deeply. When he started to raise his head to take her mouth, she held him there, begging him to drink more from her.

Taking his wrist to her mouth, he watched her as she licked the pulse there, ran her tongue over the area like he'd seen her to do his cock when she's sucked him. Feeling his climax burn up his cock, he commanded her to bite him.

His body screamed at him. As his release, more powerful than he'd ever had, was racing along his entire body, she drew hard on his wrist, drinking from him until he was dizzy with the pleasure of it. When she sealed the wounds and threw back her head again for a second, then a third, climax, he lifted her to the seat and pounded her, taking her as hard as he could as she tightened around him. When he came a final time, his body hurting from the exertion, he dropped onto her and closed his eyes.

Neither of them spoke as they tried to catch their breath. Lizzy's arms, once holding him tightly to her, hung limply as her sides, her legs lax around his waist. Logan lifted his head, using the last bit of energy he had, and looked down at her. "I want to have children with you. As soon as we can, I'd like to have as many children as we can and start as soon as possible." She smiled, but didn't move. "Lizzy are you listening to me? I would like to have a baby with you."

"How about we have one tomorrow?"

He frowned at her, thinking he'd broken her somewhere during sex.

"I'm talking about adopting a child from the place we just left, silly. His name is Jarvis Smith. He's a vampire, but doesn't know it yet."

He wondered aloud how that was even possible. He thought that there would have been someone there who would have noticed his need for blood. Lizzy didn't laugh at him as he might have expected, but told him about a child vampire.

"Vampires don't need blood or even full night until they hit twenty-five years old. Some of them later than that, but not much more. He was dropped off there as a baby and has been deemed unadoptable because of his status as bad boy. I think it's his way of trying to figure out what is wrong with him." He asked her what was wrong. "He is much like you are in learning what you can do. The hearing, the ability to see into people's thoughts and minds. He's terrified."

The car came to a halt before he could answer her or ask any more questions. As soon as the door opened, he was glad that they'd dressed so quickly after making love because Mathew had leapt at him so quickly that he barely had time to catch him before he was hugging him.

"I'm so glad you're here. I was so worried about you and scared. Grandda said it was okay to be scared, but I had to have faith in you to get yourself found. Aunt Donna and I have had three chocolate things just today."

Logan got out to be pulled into the arms of his sister.

"You certainly know how to be a pain in my ass, don't you?"

Logan kissed her again and held her as they watched Aaron standing in the doorway.

"He missed you as well. And I've never met a sharper man in my life. He knows so much about history that he makes me want to go back to school to become a history teacher."

Logan thought it was a great idea and told her so. He started to tell her that she could learn a great deal from Aaron, as the man had been around forever, when he realized she had no idea. He looked at her face then and decided as soon as this was over, he was going to have to have a long talk with her. He winked at his son as they moved up to and into the house. Aaron pulled him in for a hard hug then jerked back.

"Christ, you weren't kidding."

It took him several seconds to think what he meant, and he laughed.

"I don't think this is the least bit funny, Logan. She's my baby. I thought I made that perfectly clear."

"Yes, but I can't have a baby with her without the other part." He patted Aaron on the back. "Buck up, man. We have to finish this thing so we can get things moving in that direction."

Aaron growled, and he and Mathew laughed. Sara came around the corner and stopped a few feet away. She pointed to the stairs as she held her nose. "You smell. Get up to the bathroom now, and we'll burn those things you have on. You smell of another pack and..." She raised her nose to the air. "Do I smell burnt hair?"

Logan was still laughing as he climbed into the shower. He was scrubbing his hair when he thought of what Lizzy had said as she followed him up the stairs. They owned the buildings now. He was a full partner in the B.L.A.C.K. Corporation. He had to lean against the tile while the enormity of it rolled over him.

"You okay?"

He nodded at Lizzy before he remembered she couldn't see him.

"Logan, are you okay?"

"Yes. Fine. I was...would you like to join me in here? I could use a good back scrubbing." Her laughter made him smile. *"Is that a yes?"*

"It's a no, not until later. Everyone is downstairs waiting for you or else I would. But it's important that we find Megan more than ever. She's out there somewhere and she's not going to quit until she's captured and brought to trial."

"Trial?" He turned off the water and reached for a warm towel. *"I didn't think they'd let her be tried for her crimes here. I don't really know what I thought, but I just assumed she'd be killed on sight."*

"No. Mel will have a trial for her when she's found. Megan committed crimes against magic. Not just by using black magic, but also against a member of the royal family." She was opening drawers and came back with some pants and a t-shirt for him as she continued. "There must be a trial."

"I guess I never thought of what she did to Mel as a sort of treason. And her threats to her are nothing to be casual about either." He glanced at her as he brushed his teeth and noticed the odd look on her face. "What?"

"Logan, it's you."

He frowned at her.

"You're a member of the royal family. As my mate, you, Mathew, and Donna are royal as well. The treason was against you."

Chapter 15

Megan looked at her shop. Of course today there would be customers. Five people lined up outside, looking in windows and checking their watches. She looked at her own. Twenty-five minutes late because somehow, Lizzy and her band of wolves had come in and taken her prisoner.

And she needed to get downtown and claim her building. She wondered if they might be there waiting for her, but it would be too late. She was a land owner here, and the queen couldn't bring her to trial. She'd tried that before, but she'd gotten off with a warning that if she tried it again, she'd be toast. She wished that Sherman was still alive. He would have understood her.

Shamus, the new king, was an ass. She'd disliked him even as a child when he'd been working for Tessa. That really turned out badly for everyone when it had been discovered that not only was she a fae, but also a warrior fae and the last of her kind. Well, not anymore. She and that man had been popping out kids like it was their job. She supposed in an odd way it was. The movement across the street startled her from her memories.

A large SUV pulled up just one building down from hers. She watched as her prisoner got out, as well as Lizzy. Could a woman be more beautiful than her? There was a kid, too, the one she'd been trying to get to her last week, and Aaron and

Sara. Damn it all to hell and back. What the fuck were they doing here?

When Lizzy looked right where she was, Megan pulled the dark shadows deeper around her. Standing as still as she could, she watched as Logan moved up behind her and wrapped his arm around her. So they really were in love. How sickening.

The little boy ran up and down the street looking into windows and laughing. Megan kept an eye on him, but watched Lizzy. There was something very weird about her today. When they moved down the street to the last building on the block, she moved back into the building without taking her eyes off the group until she was out of sight.

She had a feeling that she had been felt by Lizzy, and maybe Sara. There was only one thing she could do. Actually, there were two, but the first one didn't bear thinking about so she dismissed it completely. There was no way she was going to turn herself into the queen and beg forgiveness.

First of all, she wasn't going to lie to her, not that she could, and secondly she'd be in prison long before she could get in to see her. The Guard was out to find her, and it would be just plain stupid if she were to go to Molavonta and turn herself in. She had to go with her second plan and kill the lot of them. The wolf was standing outside her hidey hole when she got close. She glanced at Ollie when he shifted and pulled on his clothes.

"Did you know that this is where the pack of the Brotherhood is?"

She shrugged.

"They don't like it when people come to their grounds without asking. I don't guess you asked him, did you?"

"Not my job. What do you care anyway? It's not like you plan to live here with him. You're here on assignment." He shook his head. "What is it? I've got things I have to take care of, and you making me play twenty questions is giving me a headache."

"I gotta go back and face the music."

She cocked a brow at him, hoping he'd explain, but he only nodded. Some days, like today, she wished to Christ she'd never found this pack. "What do you mean you have to go back or face the music? I don't know what that means. Your alpha said it was okay for me to use you as I saw fit." She felt her blood simmer when he shook his head. "Either you explain yourself so that I can understand you, or so help me, I will kill you myself."

"The alpha said that the one here is pissy on account of us being on his land. Says there are rules that need to be…" He looked thoughtful, and she wanted to tell him not to break anything when he smiled. "Said we have to follow the rules set about or there would be huge fines to pay. And I don't got the money to be paying for fines. My alpha said he ain't paying them either."

Megan was pretty sure that the fine wasn't monetary, but said nothing about that. She actually knew very little about wolves other than they liked to fuck a great deal and they were lazy. The one that Ollie had been in had an alpha that had been so fat he rolled around in one of those chairs with motors. His pack was small compared to most and as stupid as they came. She doubted anyone knew the real rules, if there were any, and decided that she wasn't going to fuck with another pack of them.

"Whatever. If you run into him or his members, just tell them to come and talk to me. I'll straighten it out with him. And if there's a fine, I'll take care of that too." She didn't have any money, but she knew that if she gave him a little pussy, as she'd done for Ollie's help, then he'd be fine. "I want you to go to my shop. There are people there and I want you to tell me what the fuck they're doing."

153

Ollie looked like he might say no, but then brightened. "We can play with them, can't we? I mean, none of us have had a good run in a few months. I'd like to be able to run me down one or two humans just to scare them a bit."

"I don't care what you do, just don't hurt Lizzy. You remember who she is, right? The blonde with the big magic." She'd rolled her at eyes at him when that's how he'd referred to her. "You hurt her, you'd better find yourself a deep fucking hole to hide in or I'll come after you."

"Nah, we won't hurt her. Can't anyway, she's marked. All of us can smell that."

She waited again for him to explain, then decided that she really didn't care enough.

After they left, she wandered around the grounds. There was enough trash around it to think it had at one time been a dump. The empty buildings, all of them in some sort of process of being built, had long since been neglected. Most of the lower spaces where glass should have been were boarded up, and even those had been broken out or had graffiti painted on them. She wondered if anything could be done to this area other than to bulldoze what was here and start over.

Going into the building she'd been working from for a long time, she looked at her collection. She'd been using the kitchen in this particular building since she'd found it. She thought it had been slated to become a restaurant at one point, and the kitchen was big enough for her to play in. She loved the fact that the freezer was the perfect place to hide people when she didn't want anyone else to be able to contact them.

It was well lined, and she had used enough of her kind of magic on it to ward it from others. The entire building had been safeguarded against others. And if things went the way she wanted, the plan she had for her building, now that she owned it, she'd be as big if not bigger than Sherman had ever dreamed for her to be. His book of spells that he'd given her just before he'd disappeared had been very helpful in her start. And now she was ready for more.

Pulling out the *Spells of White and Black*, she opened a page at random. She knew them all by heart in the back half of the book, the black magic, but she sometimes like to dabble in the white just to fuck with it until she could make it her own. It didn't ever work, but that didn't mean she didn't stop trying. Pulling up the one on how to make a tree grow made her think that she'd see if she could make it go in reverse. Going into the nearly dead grounds, it took her almost an hour to find a tree, much less one suitable to practice on, and another hour before she gave up. It was a stupid plan anyway. What the fuck did she care if a tree grew or didn't? Going back to the building, she waited on the pack to return.

~~~

"Again."

Logan glared at the man standing before him. Shamus had been working with him for nearly five hours, and he was hurting in places that he'd not known could hurt. Colin laughed when he looked at him.

"Nay, I'll not be giving you what you need either, boyo. You said to work you until you got it. The lass said for you to go slow and you said that you'd learn now. Not my fault you're as stubborn as she." Colin raised his hand and wiggled his fingers. "Like this."

Lightning shot from his fingers and singed the ground. Logan didn't leap back as he had been doing when it seemed to race toward him, but he waited. The line of blackened grass stopped an inch from his toe. As he watched, the grass seemed to heal itself over until there wasn't a trace of what Colin had just done.

Lifting up is hand, he felt the energy race along his skin, but that was the way it had done every time. But this time, he felt something more. He wiggled his fingers and felt the strong urge to raise his other hand. He did so. The arc of electricity leapt from one hand to the other and Logan held it.

"There's a boy. Now you need to use it. Think about where you'd like it to go." Colin laughed. "But don't be tossing it at us. You canna harm us, and it will come back on you tenfold."

Logan had learned that, too, when he'd unknowingly tried to pick Shamus up and toss him around liked he'd been doing to him. The way he'd bounced along the dirt had him seeing double for two hours.

"Now, Logan. Throw it at the ground now."

He did as Shamus had commanded and felt the power drain him for a second as he pushed it from him. The beauty of it, and the fact that he'd made it, made him both proud and sad to see it destroyed. He looked up when Shamus patted him on the back.

"You've done it. Of course it took you nearly a day, but you've got it now." Shamus patted him again and told him to come along. "I've something to show you. And you've a meeting with the Fates."

They went to the largest tree that Logan had ever seen. They'd been on pack property for most of the training, but Bradley had asked them to move further back from their meeting place. He had been afraid that the others would be afraid to come and ready the area for the pack meeting, and it was the night before the full moon. So they'd gone to the castle and Avalone.

"This is the tree of life. I show you this so that you'll know that magic resided in this place that is as old as time. And when you come here, to this spot, you'll know that whatever you do, whatever you feel that is magical, it comes from here. And I'd like to show you something that no one but a few have ever seen."

The area around the tree was amazing. On one side, there were fruits of every kind hanging from it, apples, oranges, and even fruits he didn't know. Another side was filled with small green buds and green branches filled with blossoms of every color. As he and Shamus moved to another quarter of the tree, he could see that the leaves had all but disappeared and that the branches now were covered in snow; the leaves and buds were gone and the grass beneath it held prints of animals that had passed by. He walked to the final side, looked at the leaves here, and saw the signs of fall, colors of gold and brown mixed with green, and Logan watched as a few of the millions of leaves dropped to the ground. He looked at Shamus.

"The tree will rotate. In a few months, the fall will be winter and the spring will have turned to summer. It will do this at each season, giving the tree life where there was none and put it to sleep in others. It is truly the tree of life."

Logan nodded.

"But that's not all it does. Come look."

He took him to the spring side and pointed to the upper branches. At first Logan wasn't sure what he was seeing until the tree seemed to bend toward him. He started to reach for the leaves there and stopped, somehow knowing that to touch was to harm and to harm what was here would never be repaired.

"She trusts you."

Logan knew that Shamus was right and laid his hand on the bark in front of him. He heard the tree sigh. "She is giving you a great gift, Logan, take it."

The leaves just in front of him seemed to flutter, and he focused on them. That's when he saw it. His breath caught when he realized what he was seeing. He watched as the leaves started to change and move. "It's my name and Lizzy's." More leaves fanned around their names and then showed his son, Mathew's, as well as several more. No names on these but one, and the rest simply said "Boy Child" and "Girl Child." He watched the ones there fan into more and more still until

Shamus called his name. As he watched, the tree branch stood again and he could no longer make them out.

"You've been shown something that others have never seen and will never know. Do you know what you've seen?"

Logan nodded as he stepped away. "I've seen my family. All of them. I've seen the children that Lizzy and I will have, and their children, and theirs as well. Mathew too. He will marry and have children as well. But not my sister."

"No, and you won't see hers either. Not here. Donna's branch is still forming. Do you know why?"

Logan shook his head but then nodded.

"You're a bright man, aren't you? Yes, Lizzy saved her life, and the branch that was to end that day for her is still reforming and becoming her own. She will live longer because of what your mate gave her, but she will eventually die. You cannot convert her; her chance at life will end when the time is right."

"Because she sort of cheated death once?"

Shamus shook his head.

"Then why can't I convert her?"

"That will be up to her own mate someday. You must listen to me, Logan. There will be a time when you want to, feel you need to, but you cannot. It is not your decision to make, nor will the Fates be happy if you do."

He nodded, trying his best to understand when three women appeared before him. Christ, he didn't think he'd get used to that ever. He bowed before them as Shamus had, then the other man disappeared. When one of them reached for his hand, he took it and found himself in a large room filled with so much color it was painful at first to see.

"We so love color, you see." Atropos smiled at him. "I can tone it down, but I'd rather not."

"No, it's your home. I would hate for someone to come to my home and ask me to change things around for them because they didn't like it. Leave it. I'll get used to it."

She smiled at him and asked him to have a seat. He sank into the most comfortable chair he'd ever been in, and felt the soreness from earlier dissipate. He looked at her when he realized one of them had done it.

"We wanted you comfortable. As a wedding gift, I'll make sure you get a set of them. Now, why we brought you here." He nodded at Clotho as she continued. "You've seen the tree. Did Shamus tell you that the only other person besides us that has been given that gift is your Lizzy? She didn't tell us until she was nearly fifty, but then she has her own powers that even we're still trying to see. She's very powerful."

"And beautiful."

They each nodded at him.

"I'm assuming that because she's my mate is why you gave me that gift as well."

"No. We didn't give you anything with the tree. It is magic all its own. What you see from her is from her only. But I believe you'll be pleased with what she has asked us to grant you."

For a reason he couldn't fathom, he was afraid. Not terrified, but just scared enough to think that what they were about to give him would change him forever. He looked at Lachesis as she continued.

"It will help you in the years to come and when dealing with Megan. She will be powerful when she finds you, so the Tree has asked us to sort of speed up your training." She handed him a drawing and he looked at the cover of a book. "She asks that you get this for the kingdom and return it. She believes that Megan stole it, or was given it by Sherman, a very powerful and evil man."

"Mel's first mate."

Clotho shook her head.

"I'm sorry. I just assumed that you were talking about him because of—"

"It's the same man, just not the mate of Mel. He tricked her, you see, all of them. We couldn't intervene because we cannot. But he served the purpose that was needed. But you do know that he's not dead, do you not?"

"He's not? I thought that...I don't understand."

Atropos smiled sadly.

"If he's still alive then how is it that Mel was able to mate with Shamus?"

"Shamus was her true mate all along. And Sherman is alive and will be for all time. He has been changed, you see. Changed into a living tree to watch and feel others around him, but unable to ever interact with them. Until now."

"Megan." Her name popped into his head almost immediately, and the sisters nodded. "She is going to set him free."

"No, she's not that powerful, but she can feed from him. The ground where she has her magic now brewing is where he is. She, of course, doesn't know this, but she can feel the power of the earth. She can harm more humans if she were to succeed in tapping into his roots. If she does that, I'm afraid many more lives will be taken."

Logan looked at the three of them. They had said they were going to speed up his training. Now he understood more. It was coming along faster than they'd thought, and he was going to be somehow helpful in bringing Megan down. He leaned back in his chair and regarded them.

"You need me."

Lachesis smiled and nodded.

"What can I get from this if I let you power me up?"

"You wish to bargain with us, Logan? Things do not always go as you wish when you make a bargain with the Fates."

He nodded, remembering from some of the movies he'd seen and the saying that he'd heard countless times. "Be careful what you wish for. I understand that. But I don't want something for myself. It's for…" He stood up to pace. "All my life I've worked very hard, most of the time going without in order to get to where I wanted to be. Not wealthy, though many think I was, but I wanted more for my family. Then my mom died a few years after I had Mathew. But I wanted Mathew to have more than me, better. Not easier, but better. Understand?"

They nodded. "You wish for him to be able to succeed."

He shook his head, knelt before the three of them, and realized that they were as beautiful as anything he'd ever seen, but nothing compared to his Lizzy. "I want you to help me find more people like me." He shook his head. "I mean beings that have a power or something that frightens them and they can find help in learning to control it. I want you to help me give them a place where they can go and feel safe secure and have someone to answer their questions."

"You wish to secure a haven for them."

He nodded. Lachesis touched his cheek, and he felt power surge through him.

"It's a deal, Logan the Warrior."

CHAPTER 16

Lizzy was in the kitchen when she felt Logan enter the house. Her body seemed to burn for him, and she went into the living room to find him standing there. He was different, more...more of everything. She waited for him to turn to look at her and saw it. She smiled. "The Fates have talked to you."

He nodded and grinned at her.

"They gave you something and you're nearly brimming over with it. How do you feel?"

"Like I've stuck my finger in a light socket and it's running through me at full blast. I've never felt so energized before." He walked toward her and she stopped him with a raised hand. "I need to touch you. If I don't, I feel like I'm going to explode."

He ran his fingers along her throat and then up and over her head. She felt the power he was giving her, and her body trembled with it. When she touched her arms, wrapped both his hands around her upper muscles, she shivered and looked at him. His green eyes were glowing.

"You know what they did to me?"

She nodded.

"I can hardly contain it. I just want to fly!"

"You more than likely can. Did you know that you've been marked? That they branded you?"

He shook his head.

"Look at your chest and tell me what you see."

He let her go with one hand, but held her with the other. As he lifted his shirt, he never took his eyes from her until she reached out and touched the mark on his chest. He looked down then back at her.

"It's the mark of the Royal Guard. And this is the mark of the royal court. But this one marks you as theirs. You're a servant of the Fates. What have you promised to do for them?" The crossed claymores were what her grandfather and mother wore; the tree of life behind it was what made him royalty. She bore the same mark, but hers was smaller, and until she'd met him, invisible to everyone but her. She would bet he could see it now if he looked. But it was the three in the fae language that she knew had made him a servant. And until he did what he'd promised them, it would remain.

"I have to find a book. A book of spells called *Spells of White and Black.* They said that Megan has it. They want me to find it."

She nodded. The book had been missing for centuries. Long before she'd been born. Her grandfather had told her that he thought Sherman had destroyed it, but apparently not. She realized then that Logan was not just powerful from something they had given him, but there was something else. When he smiled at her, she was afraid she knew.

"We're going to have a baby. We're supposed to name him Rythen. Do you know who that is?"

She nodded.

"I saw his name and no other with ours."

"You saw the Tree of Life."

He nodded.

"Who took you to it? Shamus or Mel? And why?"

"Shamus, and I don't know why. He said that the Fates wanted to talk to me, and that's where we met them. The tree showed me the rest." He frowned at her. "Are you upset about something?"

"No. Not upset. They told me that no one had ever seen what I'd seen before. I'd seen my name there with the name Rythen when I was a child. Your name wasn't there, but…" She had to sit down or fall over and went to the couch that still had the plastic covering it. "Rythen was a great warrior during the great war between the black and white users of magic. He was supposed to have ended the wars by showing the people what was going to happen to them if they continued fighting as they were. He is the being that created my grandmother, the original Queen of Magic."

"So he created Elizabeth so that she'd govern the world of magic and keep all mankind safe." She told him yes. "What happened to him? I mean, if he was that powerful then I'm assuming he couldn't die or be killed."

"He's not dead, but in the fade." He looked confused. "He's gone to sleep, sort of. There is supposed to be a fairy ring in the magical world of Avalone where he sleeps. No one knows where it is, and it's said that every few hundred years or so he wakes to make sure things are all right, then moves to another resting place. He holds some magic back. It's told that he will give to one that will succeed him."

"Do you know who that's supposed to be?"

She leaned back on the couch and closed her eyes, not answering his question.

"You have an idea, don't you?"

"I do now. I think perhaps it's the child you and I are to have. I thought that long ago, actually, but never…" She opened her eyes to look at him. "I'm not pregnant, Logan. Now that you hold power like mine, you'll know when I can get pregnant, but I'm not yet."

"We've never really talked about it. Do you want children with me?"

She smiled.

"What I've seen, and you have too, we're to have a great many children. Will that include the children that we may adopt into our homes and lives as well?"

"I don't know."

Mathew came into the room and stopped just short of leaping into his dad's arms. He stared at him for several moments before he moved slowly forward.

"What happened to you, Dad?" When he didn't answer him, Mathew looked at her. "Mom? What's going on? Did that lady come back?"

"You remember what Tristan told you about magic?" Mathew nodded. "Your dad has been given a little more. Actually, a great deal more. It'll be to protect us. Mathew, you do know that neither your dad nor I will ever harm you, don't you?"

"What a dumb question. Of course I know that." He snorted, and she decided he needed to spend less time with her dad if that's what he was teaching him. "I came down to ask if I could go over to Great-grandda's place. I wanted to show him what I figured out today in class with Pete."

Pete had come and gotten Mathew when the furniture trucks had pulled up. The two of them were going to work in his room, but when the men had started bringing in furniture, she'd asked to take him to the pack house. She'd agreed, knowing that he'd be safe there and out of the way of the movers. He'd been home about an hour and had told her how much he loved his new room.

"I don't have a problem with it. How long will you be gone?"

She looked at Logan when he asked, wondering if he realized how much time could pass for Mathew and her grandda before they knew it.

"I don't know. Mel says she's set me up a room there. Can I spend the night?"

Logan looked at her and wiggled his brows. She laughed, stood up, and walked to Mathew.

"You know the rules, right?" He nodded and rolled his eyes. "Mathew, there are things there that can hurt you. Not on purpose, but some are very big and aren't used to little guys around."

"I'm okay. Draco said that I'm a mere spit in his eye and so long as I tell him I'm in the kingdom, he'll endeavor not to squash me." He grinned. "I had to look 'endeavor' up. But I will be really careful."

They let him go, and she went back to the kitchen to put the rest of the things away that had come that morning. When he wrapped his arms around her waist, she leaned back into him. She felt his laughter.

"My son just went into another realm to talk to a being that is as old as anything I can ever imagine and was just told to be careful that a dragon not step on him. Oh, and the fairies too. We can't forget that the fairies love him to death and sit on his shoulder while he reads them stories I read to him as a child." He kissed her shoulder. "And to think I thought that I'd never have a life as good as the one I had."

She turned in his arms. "He also has a grandda that is two thousand years old who is a vampire, an aunt that is a wood nymph, not to mention uncles that change to wolves at least once a month. I think Mathew is a very lucky young man."

"I do as well. And because I'm lucky as well, how about I take you upstairs and I show you just how lucky I am by letting you help me break in our new bed?" She laughed when he gave her his puppy eyes. "I've had a very strange day and I need my mate."

She took his hand and led him to the stairs. "You do know that none of those dishes are going to be put away on their own, don't you? I expect some help when we come back down to—"

She was suddenly over his shoulder and he was taking the stairs two and three at a time. Lizzy laughed when he made a wrong turn at the top of the stairs and ended up in an empty room. She pointed to the correct bedroom and was bounced on the bed when he got to the right room.

She looked up at him from the bed and watched him as he undressed. She wanted this man with every fiber of her being and wondered how she could tell him. Sitting up slightly, she smiled at him and he paused. "I love you."

He grinned and unbuttoned the rest of his shirt.

"I want you to know that I've never loved anyone before like I do you. My life up until you came into it has been…well, not boring, but without any meaning. You've given it all to me."

"I love you too. I never dreamed in all my life…no, that's not true. I never believed I could have anyone like you. You've made me believe in love again. Given me so much that I'll never be able to convey to you how I feel." He grinned. "But if you get naked right now, I'll do my best to show you."

She stood up and crooked her finger at him to come to her. When he was standing in front of her, she reached out to take his wrist and she took his cufflinks off. When she laid them on the dresser next to them, she moved behind him and peeled the shirt down his back and to his waist.

"I'm going to buy you some t-shirts. Just plain ones that you can wear with a pair of jeans. I've never seen you in either." She ran her tongue along his spine, still holding him captive in his shirt. His moan made her need for him spike.

"I work a great deal and have never been much of a causal dresser. I've never…Lizzy, do that again, please?" He moaned again when she nipped at his shoulder. "Baby, you're killing me."

"I know. But I'm enjoying myself so just tell me why you've never worn jeans in all the time I've known you." She reached around him and unbuckled his belt one handed while he cupped her with his hands that she held behind him. "Behave, Logan, or I'll stop what I'm doing."

He stopped. Smiling, she reached into his trousers and cupped his hard cock. He rocked into her hand, and she let his arms go so that she could finish pulling his pants open. He didn't reach for her, but let her do as she pleased. When she walked around to face him, she could see his desire as his eyes had started to glow again. "You're showing through again."

He blinked at her.

"Your power won't be able to be hidden now. It's marking you for all to see. You look magnificent, powerful and strong." Lizzy licked along his mark over his heart. "I've had one similar to this one all my life. But it wasn't until now that I'm betting you could see it."

"Show me."

She nodded and started to lift her shirt over her head. He took her hands, put them over her head, and held them there. She watched him as he licked along the column of her throat and then nipped at her lobe. She was shaking she needed him so badly.

~~~

Logan could feel the power thrumming through him. The need to have Lizzy bite him was making him weak in the knees. He had no idea why now it was so important, but he could feel it. Moving his mouth along her throat to her pounding pulse, he suckled the beating vein into his mouth and held her there. Reaching behind her, he took the back of her shirt and ripped it from her. Her breath on his face made him moan.

"Logan, you're making me weak. Please, let me lay down so I don't fall."

He shook his head slightly, then lifted his head and looked down at her. She was in a mist of red, and he knew it was a beast that hid deep within him that needed her now. "No. I need you like this. I want to strip you naked and touch you in ways that will…" He unhooked her bra and lifted the material from her full breasts. "There's a thing, a beast, that needs to mark you. I don't know what it is, but I don't think he'll hurt you."

"He won't. You can control him, but I can feel him too. He wants to bite me, doesn't he?"

Logan nodded, leaned in, took her nipple into his mouth, and bit her.

"Logan, please, you have to help me."

"I will." He tore her pants from her body and she stood before him in her panties and nothing else. He gazed at her, knowing that she could feel the heat of him because of the way she was panting. Christ, he wanted her right now. When he tore his own pants from him, including his boxers, she reached out to touch him, but he shook his head at her.

"I can't let you. I need to…Christ, I need to claim you."

She nodded at him.

"Lean over the bed for me and spread your legs. I need to… I have to…" He didn't know what he needed to say, but she seemed to understand and did as he had commanded of her. As soon as she was in position, he came up behind her and fisted his cock. She moaned when he rubbed his thick head in her juices.

"I feel like I have to mate with you again. I need to mark you like I've never done before. I don't want to hurt you, but I have to…I need to hurt you." She nodded and turned to look at him over her shoulder. Her eyes were as red as he knew his to be.

When he rubbed his cock over her tight muscles of her ass, she pulled away from him. The beast, or whatever he was, didn't like that so he grabbed her by the hips and slammed deep within her. Her scream had him nearly pull out, but something within him snarled at him to finish. He leaned over her and nipped at her shoulder. "I'm sorry, baby. I'm so sorry." She nodded. "I need you. I need to come in you this way."

"Dominate me. Please, I need it too. Logan, I need for you to dominate me and claim me." As if her giving him permission was enough, he sank his fangs into her shoulder and came inside of her. Reaching to her pussy, he pinched her clit and felt her tighten around him. Lifting her up so that she rode his cock, he rested on his toes and knees as he offered her his wrist. As soon as she bit him, Logan felt the power he had within him pour from him into her. The circle, or whatever it had been, was complete.

Moving forward, he laid her on the bed and lifted from her. She lay there lax, but he could tell she was sore. Going into the bathroom, he got a warm washcloth and a towel. He went back to the bed and cleaned her up. She rolled to her back and looked up at him when he finished.

He could see her mark on her breast just above her heart. It looked just like his. When he touched it, his own burned, and he looked into her eyes.

She smiled. "We're a pair. I'm not really sure of what, but we're the same. We've given each other whatever you were given from the Fates today."

He nodded, tossed the clothes away, and lay down beside her. "There was something in me that needed to dominate you. Have you ever...I know you've never had that done to you before and I've never had the desire to do it either, but something made me want to take you that way." He held her close. "How can we find out what that was?"

"I'll have to ask someone at the castle. The three you have...well, we both now have, is from the Fates. The rest...I don't know."

He felt her fall asleep in his arms and he lay there thinking about it. He'd forgotten to tell her what else the Fates had given him, the ability to use all the power she'd given him, for one, and wondered if whatever he'd given her was something she'd just know how to use as well. He closed his eyes and thought of the child they'd have. He put his hand over her belly. He was going to love seeing her swollen with their child and knew that Mathew would as well.

Chapter 17

Bradley moved along the tree line, watching the five wolves to his left. They were his men and they weren't very happy with him right now. Well, tough shit. He was going on this hunt, and they could very well get over it or go home. He had promised Aaron that he'd make sure that the woman and her wolves were no longer a threat, and he was damn well going to do it. A movement out of the corner of his eye made him pause. Then he started cussing.

"I thought I told you to stay home."

Airic growled low at him as she came up beside him.

"Damn it, woman. You might get hurt."

"So might you. Besides, since when have I ever listened to you when you ordered me around like one of our cubs? Never. So I'll tell you now, shut the fuck up and let's get this taken care of so we can go home. I've got a kiln I have to turn up in three hours, and I don't want this thing to get in the way of it."

He thought about telling her to go back again, but didn't want to embarrass himself. She would roll him and show him who was boss again, and he didn't want to have to go through the ribbing again. Smiling to himself, he thought of the payback he'd give her later and decided that it might just be worth it to tell her, but something in front of them moved. Everyone, including her, stilled and dropped down to the ground.

"There are seven of them. One female and the rest males."
Bradley nodded at his brother David.

"They can't be more than a few years older than my oldest."

"But they were warned to stand down or else." Bradley had spoken to their alpha again, and had been assured that the leader of this group of rogues had been told to come home two days ago. Now they were in direct violation of the pack laws that had been handed down from generation to generation for as long as there had been weres. He reached for the leader, a man by the name of Ollie Wright, and felt the connection immediately to him and his group of wolves. *"You are on pack land that you've no permission to be on. I've spoken to your alpha, and he claims that you've been ordered home and that fines will be paid."*

The leader stepped out of the shadows. Bradley was pretty sure he couldn't see them yet, and thanks to Sara, he wouldn't be able to scent them either.

"You have the wrong information. We are with a female of great power and she said that we have her permission by order of the queen of..."

Bradley watched him turn and another wolf came to stand beside him.

"Queen of magic. She called her to be here."

Bradley felt the stir of magic around them, and then Mel was standing before them. His men knew her and lowered their eyes from her as a show of respect. Mel was one hell of a woman and sweet as could be, but when a person fucked with her, she was as mean as his grandmother had been when she was on a roll.

"Do you know who I am?" Mel asked the wolves in front of her as they stood still in the light of her magic. None of them moved to either bow or to step forward.

"You're the queen, I suppose, but you've no claim over us. Our female said that you were all puff and not much in the way of magic. But she did say that you gave her permission to find the woman and her male." Ollie sat down and yawned before he continued. *"She said to tell you if you had a problem with us being here to come talk to her and she'll straighten you out."*

Bradley nearly laughed when Mel turned to look at him. Ollie had dismissed her as if she were nothing. Her face said that she was pissed, but her body language said she was as relaxed as she could be. Shamus shimmered beside her and looked over the pack of wolves. When he stepped forward, Bradley went with him. Airic stood just in front of Mel to protect her if need be. As soon as Shamus spoke, Bradley knew that he'd be able to hear what was being said to Shamus from any of the other wolves.

"This is Bradley Wolfe, alpha of the Brotherhood of the Gray, the largest pack in the world. Have you heard of him?"

Ollie yawned at Shamus as he spoke to them.

"I see. You're incredibly stupid. You know that, don't you?"

"Stupid? Nah, I don't think so. But I've seen our female's magic, and she's got it all together. You and that queen over there have put her here without cause and she just wants her payback."

Shamus nodded.

"So if you guys don't mind, we gotta find the woman called Lizzy and a man by the name of Logan. I think you might know where they are."

"Yes, we do." Shamus crossed his arms over his chest and smiled. "And you can have her on one condition. Just one, but you all must agree to it."

"A condition, huh? Well, I'm not so sure about that. The female we work with has sort of got us all tied up in conditions right now. I don't know if we can take on any more."

Shamus leaned down to face the wolf eye to eye. "You give over and I won't have these wolves behind me kill you. Because no matter what Megan has told you, you're going to get your asses killed if you go near my friends. Not that I think you can take them either, but…" Shamus shrugged. "Would you like a little taste of what they can do to you?"

The wolf looked at him. Bradley knew what Ollie saw—an older wolf with a little gray at his muzzle. What he didn't know—and wouldn't until it was too late—was that he had a great deal of magic within his blood, some of it from the man he stood beside. The wolf nodded that he wanted more proof, and Bradley leapt.

He had the other wolf down and his canines deep into his throat. A sharp move or even a slight one would have him bleeding. Bradley had a feeling that it wasn't going to end well for the leader of this small pack. Shamus laughed when Ollie whimpered.

"You are stupid. Did you really think because of his apparent age, he would wait for you to say anything? This man is a great leader among his men and has survived many attacks much larger than this one and has come out the winner." Shamus ran his hand over his fur. "If I release him from you, will you leave this area now?"

"No."

Before the word was out of his mind and into Bradley's, he tore his throat out. Shamus stepped back as the rest of his pack attacked the rogues. It was over within minutes. He walked beside Airic and sat beside the queen as Shamus turned toward them. All seven of the others were dead and his men were unharmed.

"This was a great loss for our kind, Bradley. Thank you for making it quick."

Bradley nodded.

176

"You'll have to find Megan now. But only find her. Lizzy will need to deal with her, don't you think, Mellie?"

"Yes. This war that she opened is between the two of them now."

When she ran her hand over Bradley's head, he felt a surge of power that nearly knocked him over.

"For what you've done for me."

She disappeared along with Shamus a few minutes later. Bradley looked around at the carnage and then at his mate. She was smiling.

"She has all the power in the world and then some and can't ever clean up the mess she leaves behind. Why is that, you suppose?"

Airic snorted.

"Just so you know, you got whatever she gave me too."

"I know. I feel younger already." She stood up and started away, then stopped and turned back to him. *"If you hurry up and get this cleaned up, I'll make it worth your while, alpha. I have a powerful need to run with you, and if you're a very good boy and don't bitch overly much about this mess, I'll let you take me any way you want."*

She ran off in the direction of their house, and Bradley turned back to David with a grin. He was looking at the bodies that had to be dealt with. As much as he wanted to run after his mate and play, he wasn't that sort of leader. He shifted when the others did, and dressed.

Gathering the bodies took more time than he thought it would, but they had found things on the bodies, marks that had caused them pause. When Bradley had asked for Shamus or Mel to come back to see them, they had brought in Phillip as well. The marks were of black magic. These men had been marked by magic that none of them had seen in a very long time.

"It's Megan's mark. Just like the one she left before we'd asked her to leave the kingdom. She's been practicing on these

177

wolves in a dangerous way." Phillip stared down at the female that had been mutilated not in the attack, but by a magic that had left her deformed and scarred.

Most of them had been burned badly by magic; a few of them had been permanently changed to a wolf. The leader had been harmed in such a way that had he lived, he would never have fathered a child. She'd hurt him that badly.

"I'll take care of them. We cannot bury them in the forest or it will die trying to heal from this." The bodies were suddenly gone and Mel turned to him. "I've contacted Lizzy and Logan. They're aware of what had happened here. I would ask that you and two of your most trusted men go with them when they confront Megan. I've asked Colin, as well as Aaron and Kyle to go. A show of force, if you will."

"Will they be able to defeat her?"

Mel nodded at David's question.

"Then I should like to be there with them. I may not be able to help much, but if you need a show of force then I would be honored to go."

Mel nodded and then looked at Bradley. "You must go as well. But I will speak to your mate. It isn't as if I think she can't handle herself, but I would like for her to stay with Sara. She won't like not being able to help her daughter."

"I understand." And he did. When his own daughter had been hurt a few months back and Mac had saved her for him, he'd been nearly insane wanting to be with her. But he would have been irrational, and that wouldn't have helped anyone.

Bradley started back for his home and wondered what had happened that this had become so bad. He'd heard stories about the woman who'd gotten her father killed and her mother nearly mortally wounded, but not everything.

Shamus appeared beside him as he walked. "The story told is that the royal guards were there to protect the queen, and Megan's father was killed in the process. Her mother had been wounded as well by one of the men that are always there to protect the queen. This was before I mated with Mellie, but I have heard it from her, not the rumors. Would you really like the story?"

Bradley nodded. He liked this king. He was personable and very friendly. And he loved his mate as she deserved to be loved. Mel and Shamus ran a good kingdom, and the two of them had five children, three girls and two boys, that showed how much they loved their lives as a truly mated couple. Shamus smiled when Bradley turned to him to ask him about the surge he'd felt.

"If you wish, you may have more children. She gave you a gift of life for both you and your mate."

Bradley grinned.

"You would like the story or your mate now, Bradley the Alpha?"

He glanced in the direction of his home and knew that when he got there, the gift would still be theirs to use. He looked back at the king and knew that if they were to finish this, it would be important to know what they were doing it for.

"Megan had been tutored by Sherman to be a great mage. The problem was that she got greedy and he got stupid with her powers. It is rumored that he gave her the book of spells. He had stolen it from Phillip and had been using it with Megan to change what was in it. The spells of black were something that should never have been written down, but Phillip said that he wanted to be able to reverse whatever they had been used upon. Without the spell, it would be impossible to repair the damage."

"Sort of like a mix of wires. Once they were tangled, you'd need the color codes to figure out which ones you'd tied off incorrectly."

Shamus nodded.

"I can see that, I suppose."

"But it fell into the wrong hands and she had been using it in the dark forest. There had been life there before then; trees flourished grandly and the fairies and brownies kept the trees as well as the blossoms bright and growing. But Megan had destroyed all but a few acres of the forest, and with it, any chance of it growing back. By the time it was discovered what she'd done, it was too late. So Mellie summoned her parents and told them she must be made to stop or she would have no choice but to send them all away."

"She didn't stop."

Shamus shook his head.

"How did her parents really die? She killed them, didn't she?"

"Yes, I'm afraid she did. When Megan stepped forward to confront Mellie, the Guard stepped in front of her. Megan raised her hand and tried to slice the two guards in half, but only succeeded in killing her own father. When he fell dead, her mother had grabbed her to try and stop her, but she only tossed her away and Delilah had ended up landing badly on a sword of one of the injured guards. When Mellie tried to help her, Megan grabbed her arm, and Mellie's protection, something that is there in her blood as it is mine, it tore the child's arm off."

Shamus stopped talking, but Bradley knew there was more to the story.

"Mellie tried to repair her so that she wouldn't have to try and survive without an arm, but Megan hadn't been grateful at all. She spit in Mellie's face and told her she'd kill her the next time she saw her. And not only that, but three members of the Royal Guard had been hurt and had to retire after. It was a huge blow to Mel and the kingdom."

"So she ended up here after all, and now she blames this on Lizzy. I don't understand how she's able to blame anyone but herself for this."

"Lizzy was there. She was sitting in the court with her mother, Sara. When Lizzy ran forward to save Megan's mother, Megan tried to hurt her. Mellie saved her as Lizzy saved the woman. In Megan's eyes, Lizzy had been sucking up, and my Mellie had never seen the real Lizzy."

They stood outside his home, and Bradley looked around the yard as he thought about what he'd been told. "So all these years, she's seen Lizzy as her nemesis. Someone that she had to prove herself against."

"Pretty much." Shamus nodded to the woods behind his home. "When this is over, you'll need to expand your lands. I would say that the man next to you is willing to sell to you for a price. Would you absorb his pack into yours? It will be more than a few more for you to rule."

More pack meant more work. Not that he was afraid of it, but he wasn't getting any younger. He started to tell him no, that he just couldn't do it, but Shamus put his hand on his shoulder. Bradley looked at him.

"I would not ask this of you if I wasn't sure you could handle it."

Bradley snorted.

"Okay, maybe I would, but the pack is dying and without leadership such as yours, it will. There will be money to add to the coffers if you do this. And land, nearly double what you have now."

He eyed him sharply. "I have nearly ten thousand acres now and almost that many in my pack. It's a great deal more than a few if there is that much land to come with it. How many, Shamus, and why me?"

"Mellie said you were a suspicious man and that you'd ask before saying yes or no." He sighed heavily. "Nearly five thousand wolves, and you because there is no other that can bring them to heel. If you don't take them, the one that takes charge will bring them down. When he does, Mellie and I will have no choice but to destroy them all. It's not what we want.

They will attack the kingdom when they come together because they'll think that we're the cause of their misfortune. I ask you this as a friend."

"You ask a great deal." Bradley watched the trees sway in the breeze then the swing on the set in his yard move. "There will be problems, as you know, and the money is not the least of my concerns, but it will help. I'll have to speak to Airic to see what she has to say, but I'm pretty sure I know already. When will this happen?"

"Soon," he told him. "Very soon."

CHAPTER 18

"I don't understand. What do you mean they're all gone? I just sent them out on a mission and now I can't find them." Megan's head hurt, and she was standing in the middle of the street talking on a payphone. She glanced around, uncomfortable being out in the open talking to the alpha.

"As I have told you four times now, they are gone. I spoke with Ollie four days ago and told him that he either had to return to me or there was going to be hell to pay. Then just yesterday morning, I spoke with him again and he said that you had taken care of the problem with the other alpha and that they were set to stay." He sighed and spoke to her as if she were nothing more than shit on his shoes. "You fucked up, and now they're gone. All of them that came with you are dead."

The line went dead and she hung up. She would have called him back, but she didn't even have the money to do that. She looked at her building and decided that she'd waited long enough for them to come tell her she was the new owner. She went to the back door. She needed things from the apartment and she wasn't getting them waiting on the stupid person downtown to tell her it was hers. But her key didn't work.

Over and over she tried it until she just pushed her power into the lock and watched as it melted away. She'd have to have that fixed soon, but for now, she would put a ward on it and that would be that. But that wouldn't work either. She finally had to enter the building and push a large box in front of it so nothing could simply get in. She moved to the store front and stopped.

Everything was gone. Her herbs and spices, even her small jars in the windows that she'd collected over the years were gone. She looked for her cash register and found it, too, was missing. Hurrying to the stairs, she went up to find that it had been ransacked, and all her things, while there, had been put into large trash bags and put near the stairs. Even her things in the bathroom were gone. She sat on the floor and tried to think what the fuck had happened.

Someone had robbed her. Or they were trying to rob her. She went back downstairs and tried to find anything that would give her a hint as to what had come in and thought they could take her things. That's when she saw the note attached to the front door. Opening it, she pulled the paper off, closed the door behind her, and stood there reading the two sheets of paper.

It took her three tries to realize just what it said. A company by the name of B.L.A.C.K. now owned her building and the ones surrounding hers. She couldn't think who they might be, but she knew where she could find out. She went to the bedroom again to find something clean to wear and found a towel. She took a long, hot shower, her first in a week, and pulled on clean clothes. It was time to go and find someone at the courthouse that could help her. Just as she stepped out of the bathroom, she screamed.

There were ten of them. She might have been impressed had she had time to think about it, but they had her wrapped in irons and held between them before she could guess their intent. When the Royal Guard parted, Lizzy stood by the door. Megan tried to attack the fucking bitch, but got no further than the links of chain would allow her.

184

"Megan, daughter of Dahlia and Izic, Fairies of the North Field, I hereby take you into custody to be brought to trial by the—"

"You can't take me into custody. You've no rights. That is for the queen to decide, and since she isn't here then…" The small room seemed to shift and move, then the queen was standing there. The guards stood straighter and held her just a little tighter. The queen kissed Lizzy on the cheek before she looked at her.

"Hello, Megan. You've been a very bad girl again. What do you have to say for yourself?" Megan said nothing. "I see. Take her back to the kingdom and place her in a cell. I want her chained and her room warded against her magic."

"You can't do that." She flushed when the queen looked at her. "You can't lock me away. I know the rules, and it says so long as I'm making my own way I can't be brought to you for crimes I…you think I've committed."

"And what is it exactly that you've been doing to make your own way?" The queen looked around the room then back at her. "You're a squatter here, and you've no lease to say that you can rent this place from the owners. What is it that you have done?"

"I own the building as of the day before yesterday. I placed a bid, and now that I own it, I don't have to pay rent."

The queen looked thoughtful, then turned to her. "You'll need to be present at the trial to end this. As soon as proof of your ownership can be found, I will set you free. Until then, you—"

"I can't get to the courthouse. I've not been able to…" She tried to rein in her temper when Lizzy leaned in to say something to her but Megan cut her off. "I need to get to the courthouse."

"I'll take care of that for you. Is there anything else you require before I set the date?" The queen waited and Megan wanted to tell her that if she'd go now, she wouldn't have to waste time on setting anything up, but she kept her mouth shut and shook her head. "Take her to the dungeon and lock her in."

Suddenly, she was being shoved into a dark cell. The four men who had brought her here held their swords on her as two more chained her to the wall. The younger one looked at her as the towel she still had on slipped a little more. When she tried to make it fall more, Marcus, the same guard that had taken her and her mother out of the kingdom, barked the boy's name.

"Daniel. Come away from her before she slits your throat."

He leapt back so quickly that he hit the wall behind him before he could scramble away from her.

"She's a black spider, and will coil you into her web so quickly you won't know you're hurt until it's too late."

She was chained to the wall within minutes and clothes were wrapped around her. She looked up at Marcus and sneered at him. He chuckled as if he had not a single thing to do with her parents' death. Before she could cast a spell at him, she felt the ribbon of magic cover her mouth.

He leaned down and looked at her. "You've got yourself well and truly caught now. Your parents were good people who I miss daily. They should have done as the queen asked and sent you away to be raised by others instead of losing their lives to save your worthless self." She glared at him, unable to say what she really wanted to. He stood up and backed out of the cell. But he wasn't finished.

"The trial is set for the day after tomorrow. You'll be given a fair trial, not that you deserve it, but the queen is a fair lady." When she growled, he laughed. "'Twill do me the best of good to see you hanged for your crimes if for none other than the fact that you've lived this long."

The door slammed shut after him, and she felt the magic sealed her mouth loosen. She wasn't free to speak her mind, but she could easily breathe now. Looking about the cell, she wondered who had made the improvements and knew that they'd done this for her. Leaning her head back against the wall, she smiled when she thought of their faces when they went to the courthouse and found that she did own the building. She was going to make them pay.

The small fairy stone was slid beneath the door, and she held her breath as it moved nearly to her before it came to a stop. She had to angle her body in a near pretzel-like position before she could blow across it. As it formed, she wondered who had sent her such a gift and watched as its owner came to life.

The tiny fairy stretched her wings. The color of the green grass, the fairy fluttered her wings as she looked at her. When she walked toward her, Megan started to smile, but stopped when she felt the sharp pain in her thigh. "What the fuck was that for?"

The grass fairy smiled as she jabbed her again.

"Stop that. What do you think you're doing?"

"You're the one, are you not?" The fairy flew to her lap and walked up her belly to her breast to stand on the rough material that she'd been clothed in. "You're Megan the Black, are you not?"

The title pleased her, but before she could tell her anything, the fairy stabbed her again. This time, Megan could see what it was she was using. It was a thorn tipped in black.

"You've taken everything from my family, and now you're here to stand trial. You've no idea how long we've waited for this."

Megan tried to blow her off, but she only landed near her leg again.

"I'll not be able to kill you as I wish, but I can take from you a little of what—"

"Lawna." The voice through the door startled them both. "Come out of there this minute."

Megan couldn't see the man on the other side, but she knew the voice. Logan was going to set her free, she just knew it. She looked at the grass fairy and smirked. With one more deep stab to her thigh, the little person went to the door and waited for it to be opened. He stood there in the opening, smiling down. Megan refused to believe it was for the little green thing and watched him as he leaned down to speak to her.

"Who let you in here?"

Lawna stomped her foot.

"I see. Being stubborn. That's all fine and dandy, but what do you suppose would have happened if the queen had found you?"

"She would have been very angry with me. She said that I was to behave while she…" Lawna turned to Megan and glared. "I don't like her."

"Not many do. But that is no reason for you to be in here sentencing her before her trial. Right?"

Lawna looked at her again before fluttering her wings and landing on Logan's finger he had put out for her.

"My son is looking for you. He said that you were going to teach him the way of the seed. May I come along?"

The door shut between them before Megan could speak to Logan. She called his name, but he didn't return. After a few minutes, she leaned back against the wall and wondered why she was being treated like this.

As soon as they found her paperwork, she was going to be set free. Then she'd show them all what she was really like. Moving her legs in front of her, she looked at the small chain on her ankle and smiled. If only they knew what the little charm held. Watching it twinkle in the light from the window, she thought of the plans she had for the book now hidden there.

"I'll show them what a person of my talent can do with such a thing." Megan rolled her foot so that the charm was lying flat against her skin. She saw that if she looked close enough, she could see the title. And knew that soon she'd be able to leave here with it.

~~~

Logan was exhausted. They'd been over the apartment four times…and nothing. Then when they'd found her second bolt hole, they'd gone over it at least a dozen times. It just wasn't here. He sat down on the steps to the apartment and decided he was too tired to think. He looked up when Lizzy sat next to him.

"We can try again tomorrow. I don't know about you, but I don't think I can look around in her nasty crap again tonight." He pulled her to him and held her. "Logan, do you suppose she never had it in the first place?"

"I don't know. But I think the Fates think she does, and they gave me this boost to find it." Or at least he thought that's what they'd done. For all he knew, this could be another wild goose chase. He looked at the roll off trash dumpster that had been delivered that morning. "We haven't even put anything in it in the event that it might be hidden in something we can't see. I'm so afraid of failing them." He didn't know what would happen if he failed, and he was pretty sure he didn't want to find out.

He watched Lizzy roll the ring he'd given her this morning around her finger. As if she felt him ready to explain that he'd get her a nicer one again, she turned in his arms to look up at him. "I wouldn't trade this one for all the money in the world. It's perfect." She stood up. "Now, we have to go home. The trial is in the morning and I, for one, am looking forward to it. Come on, we'll read Mathew a story and go to bed."

He walked with her to the car and thought about the book again. He knew that it was with Megan and that she had hidden it in a spell or something. He climbed into their new car and drove back to the house. He thought about what Lawna had told him yesterday.

"She's got magic but she can't use it here," Lawna had said.

"I don't understand. What kind of magic and where does she get if from?" He thought about his question and revised it. "You said she has it but you don't say how she has it."

"The castle. It's powerful all by itself to protect the queen and king. Any magic that isn't yours isn't used."

He had to think about that and thought he had it by the time he'd taken her to where Mathew was by the pool. "You mean if I came here with pure magic that I was born with, that's the only magic I could use?"

"And the room where the trial will be held will render all magic useless." She looked thoughtful. "Well, except for one. There was Sam. Her mind was her magic, and the queen wasn't able to take that away without harming her. Sam can do much with her mind."

So an empath could use her magic. Logan didn't have a clue why that seemed important, but he kept coming back to that. He looked over at Lizzy as they neared their home. "Are you an empath?"

"Yes I am. Why do you ask?" She smiled at him and he could see her exhaustion. "Are you planning a big take over and need to control someone?"

"Lawna said that Sam was an empath and that she could use her magic in the courtroom. Can you?"

"Yes. But you do realize that you're an empath as well. And as a member of the courts, you could use any magic so long as you don't aim anything at Mel or Shamus. What are you thinking?"

He wasn't sure and told her that. "But I have a feeling that Megan has the book on her somewhere. I know she was searched, but there is something too... She just acts like she's untouchable."

190

"It would have to be small and coated in a mixture of silver and gold. Her magic can be hidden behind that, but I don't think she's strong enough to hold it. Someone else could have given her the book hidden behind that sort of magic. She would be able to open it, but not…"

He looked over at her when she stopped talking. He waited, knowing that she was working something out or speaking to someone else. He pulled into the driveway and sat with her. Sara came out of their house with Mathew at her side. She'd been watching him for them. When Lizzy turned to look at him, he smiled back at her.

"I might have an idea where she got the book and how she's hiding it. I have to talk to Lawna in the morning. She's putting the grass to bed and will be in the courts tomorrow."

He nodded as he got out. Fairies put the flowers to bed at night and woke them with kisses in the morning. He'd seen them do it. Otherwise, even with all the other things he'd seen, this would be hardest for him to believe. Millions of them flew over the fields spreading dewy drinks and kissing them. Their colors were so brilliant it nearly hurt his eyes to watch them. Then at night under the light of the fireflies that did the same, they gave them a drink then kissed them to sleep. It was the most beautiful thing he'd ever seen.

After putting Mathew to bed, they went to their room. Most of their things were still in boxes that they'd bought them in. Bags lined the walls of more things. The only rooms that were completely set up were the kitchen out of necessity and Mathew's room. The living room had furniture, but it wasn't in any sort of order, and the television that they'd bought was still sitting in the box on the floor, the hanger to hold it on the wall in place, but nothing else. Their dining room was a shambles of empty and full boxes, chairs sitting atop one another, and a large table that was so covered in framed pictures, plates, and stereo equipment that he had no idea what it looked like. He sat on the bed and nearly fell asleep.

"Logan, lay back and I'll strip you down."

He heard her voice, but was nearly too out of it to think what she was saying to him.

"Lay back."

He felt her hand on his shoulder and let her lay him back. He opened his eyes twice when Lizzy said his name, but other than an occasional grunt, he said nothing to her. When he felt the covers over him, his entire body went limp, and then nothing more.

Chapter 19

Lizzy watched her mom. She'd agreed to help her with this and seemed genuinely excited about it. As she came out of the cell after getting Megan ready for the trial, Genese turned to wink at her. She looked like she'd found what they needed.

The little fairy had been her friend since she'd been a child. She'd also spent some time with her mom when she'd been held in these same cells a very long time ago. She had been a spy for them all night. Lizzy just hoped that it was something they could use. As much as she loved the little person, she could be a tad on the annoying side when she was onto something.

As the troop of guards walked by her hiding place, Genese flew from her mom's shoulder to hers. As soon as the others were clear, she spoke to Lizzy. It took her ten minutes to calm down.

"She's nuts. I'm not kidding you, Lady Lizzy, she believes herself to be above all this because she was thrown from the kingdom unjustly. Unjustly, she thinks? I was there. I saw what she did to her poor parents. If I would have said those things to my own mother, she'd tan my hide good. I'd not be able to sit for a month. And when I did, it would have to be on the softest petals. I have a bed made of daisy petals. They are so soft and warm. I would have loved a rose petal to cover with, but they—"

"Genese."

The little fairy snapped her mouth closed with a smile.

"You find anything in there other than the fact that she's nuts?"

"Oh aye, my lady. She has a scent on her that is weak, but I can smell him. The one who is the tree." She'd said this so softly because she, like most of the smaller beings that lived there, was afraid that Sherman would return someday and make them all pay. "She has a bit of his magic on her."

That's what Lizzy had thought. Before she could ask her where she'd found it, Genese told her that they should go. She started down the hall toward the courtroom and went to sit with the rest of her family. She was glad that Mathew was in school. This might just be too much for him to hold as a secret.

There was every living being in the room. Some even spilled out into the halls and on the lawns surrounding the room. Lizzy knew that they had come to see how the woman who'd killed her own father had fared. And to see justice done. Mel and her grandmother were seated with several other members of the court, and the Fates sat in the row in front of the table. The stand where Megan stood was surrounded by Tess and her men.

Megan did look like she was above this. She looked like she was bored almost, and that she had better things to do than to stand here with all of them. When she looked at her, Lizzy could feel her hatred as if she was touching her with it, and Lizzy shivered from it. When Logan took her hand, she felt much better.

Mel called the courts to order, and Megan was told to stand and listen to her crimes. She stood slowly and yawned before she finally looked at Mel and the rest of them. Mel wasn't amused.

"You're brought here today to face the crimes of treason against the royal family, theft of property of the kingdom, murder of a being, using dark magic when—"

"I did not murder anyone."

The courtroom murmured when Megan cut off the queen.

"You can't charge me for something I had nothing to do with. Those wolves were killed by another pack, not by me."

"You were warned, were you not, that they were on other pack alpha's land? And you were told that they were to leave the property immediately and that fines were to be paid." Megan nodded, but before she could speak, Mel held up her hand. "You'll not interrupt me again, Megan the Black, or so help me I'll make you regret it."

Megan closed her mouth and Mel continued. The list was long as she named each member of the pack that had been killed and their ages. Most, Lizzy realized, were pups not much older than twenty-five. After Mel named each member, she asked their former alpha to stand and repeat what he'd been told by alpha Wolfe.

"He told me that if I didn't bring them home, it was within his rights to kill them." The man pulled at his collar. "I told him that he could have them. That I had washed my hands of them. I also told him that if there were fines to be paid, that the woman here owed them to him."

He pointed at Megan, who stood up, but sat back down quickly when Tess turned to her with her blade drawn. Several people laughed, and that seemed to make Megan more pissed. When she sat down, Lizzy watched her as she played with a chain around her ankle.

"As for the use of dark magic in the new world, there are crimes against nature and one of the royal family within those crimes. With your sentence of being barred from here, you were expressly forbidden to use any magic at all that wasn't your own. And as you had none when you left here, any and all magic was against the law." Mel pulled out a file and looked down at it before looking at Megan again. "Do you have anything to say before I list these crimes against you as well?"

"Yes. You've no right to keep me here. I'm a land owner of my own right, and as your own rules state, I'm human and can't be tried here." She stood up. "You said you'd look into that for me. Was that another lie, or did you find my statements to be true?"

"You know as well as anyone in this room that I cannot lie. And as I said I'd take care of looking into it for you, I did. There are no records indicating that you own anything. No land, not even an apartment that has your name on any of the records that I could find."

"You do lie or you fixed it so that I was erased from the records." When she tried to move toward Mel every warrior surrounding her drew their swords, but Megan was blind to that in her fury. "Logan was supposed to go there and make his claim, but he didn't, and that woman at the courthouse said that if he didn't show, my bid would be next. He wasn't there."

"And where was he if not there? How do you know that he didn't show up and make his claim? Were you there?"

Lizzy held her breath, hoping that Megan would confess.

"You seem so sure of yourself, Megan, or is this another one of your puffed up stories?"

"He was with me when the time came. He couldn't have been there because I had him chained to the wall in my basement. I wasn't there either because I was with him, making sure that I could win against him and Lizzy."

The room became silent and when her dad nodded to her, Lizzy stood up, walked to the table, and handed the file she'd held to Mel. With a quick wink, she turned to face the crowd. "My mate had come to an agreement with my father and his group. They had signed off on a partnership the day before, and in doing so, made Madison Dixon, lawyer for the firm of

B.L.A.C.K., able to represent Logan. She was able to secure the buildings on that—"

"No. No, that's not right." Megan pulled on the bands on her arms and tried to get at her. "You're a fucking liar. All of you are. I own that building and I can't be tried here. This is not right. I'm better than all of you."

"Really? And how is that possible?" Lizzy watched the rage slide over Megan like a warm blanket and egged her on more. "You think you have some special power that makes you better than us? I don't believe you. You were a brat as a child, and you're a horrible being now. Nothing you could say or do now will change any of that."

"Sherman didn't think so." The room grew eerily quiet, but Megan was beyond listening. "He loved me and told me so. He said that if he'd ever had a child, he wished she could be just like me. He gave me things, gifts that my mother made me return. But I hid the best away and you'll never get it from me."

Her laughter was maniacal and loud. As Logan stood up, Lizzy looked at him, sorry for the insanity of the woman who held the one thing he was looking for. But he pointed at her finger and then nodded to her. She lifted the ring he'd given her to show him and he smiled and nodded. Then she looked at Megan.

It took her several seconds to realize what he was saying, and she moved toward Megan smiling. Christ, she had it on her the whole time. And Genese had known it. Before she was close enough to touch, Tess stepped in front of her.

"I can't let you near her, Lizzy. She could harm you and I can't allow that."

Lizzy nodded and looked at Tess with a smile.

"I really hate that look," Tess said.

"She has something that belongs to Phillip. Could you—" Lizzy felt Logan step up beside her and wrap his arm around her waist. "He could get it, couldn't he? It's the charm around her ankle."

Tess looked at Megan then back at Logan. "You'll do just what I tell you and nothing more?"

He nodded.

Within seconds, Megan was being held down and her screams were tearing through the room. When Tess nodded at Logan, he reached forward and started to grab the charm from her ankle when Phillip was suddenly beside him.

"Don't touch it."

They both looked at her grandfather.

"It's spelled to kill any who touch it while it's on her body."

Tess laughed. "Touch it, you say? Well, we can handle that. Men, hold this bitch down. I've something of a project to take care of." Her blade glistened in the light and as it came down, Lizzy turned her head into Logan's chest and he held her. The scream that accompanied the clash of metal against metal nearly made her sick. When Logan laughed, she looked up at him.

~~~

Logan walked to Phillip and bowed before him. He'd gone to the Fates first to give them the small charm, but after they'd inspected it and claimed it to be the right book, they gave it to him to do as he pleased. Since he wasn't sure what to do with it, giving it to Phillip seemed to be the best bet. As soon as it was in his hand, the chain fell away and the book lay before them on the table.

"She had it the entire time?"

Logan had no answer to Phillip's question so he didn't say anything.

"Sherman had asked me about it many decades ago and, like a fool, I told him what it was."

"Not a fool, sir, but a man who trusts easily. I've been accused of that myself a very long time ago. I closed up my heart, never to share it again because of that one comment." Logan pulled Lizzy to him. "But now I have reason to love and trust again."

They looked at the woman still screaming on the floor. Tess was still laughing, and he had to grin himself. When she'd brought the blade down, everyone, including himself, had thought she was going to take her head off, or the very least Megan's leg. When the blade hit the metal of the chain, it broke and fell away without much in the way of fanfare. For a few seconds anyway. The magic that came from the chain flared high in the room before it came to rest on the tip of Tess's blade. She looked at him and nodded.

The power that surged through him nearly knocked him on his ass, and when he reached for Lizzy, he felt it run from him to her like a long line of electrical conduit. The two of them fell to the floor, their breath knocked from them.

"How are you feeling now?" Tess had come up behind them as she put her sword away. "You should get yourself something to drink. Juice is good, but a little blood may not be remiss."

She winked at them as she walked away. She followed her men out of the room and to the courtyard where Megan was going to be hanged. With her possession of the book of spells and her crimes against Logan, her sentencing was quickly over.

Logan looked at Mel. "Will you be all right?"

Mel nodded and smiled sadly.

"She won't be bothering you again, Mel. You had to keep the kingdom safe."

"I thought the same thing of Sherman once he was gone, but he seems to keep coming back all the time. Do you think there will ever be a time when he's not coming back to bite me in the ass?"

Logan looked at Shamus when he sat beside Mel. "I don't know that much about him other than he was a prick and an asshole. I'd say that you have the best now, a king who loves you, parents that support you, and a family that would do anything for you. It could be a great deal worse."

"Really? And how is that, Logan? I'm nearly as old as the world, I work all the time, and I have no life to call my own. Not that I don't love what I do and the people who come to me for advice, but a break once in a while might be fun."

He knew she was kidding and laughed with her. She quirked her brow when he didn't answer right away. Then he glanced at Aaron. "You could have him as your father-in-law." He pulled Lizzy to him as Aaron came toward him. "And be mated to the man's only daughter."

Mel laughed, and Aaron glared. The two of them had been bickering for nearly the entire time he'd known them. But he also had noticed that while they seemed to not be able to stand one another, he knew that either of them would die for the other. There was a great deal of love and respect there.

Lizzy hugged them all as she told them goodbye. They had to get their house in order, and he had to get to work. The first meeting of the group of men he now could call partners was tonight after sunset, and he was looking forward to it. And since Aaron had volunteered his home, he and Lizzy had to get to it.

They walked along the walkway to their front door and stopped when they saw Bradley on the front porch sitting in a swing they didn't own. Airic was with him. They both stood up when they joined them.

"We heard the meeting was here and came to see if we could help you." Airic nodded toward the truck in the drive. "We brought some food too."

Logan grinned. "You know that we haven't opened anything. The television isn't even hung on the wall yet."

"Yeah, we got that." Bradley nodded behind them and smiled. "I brought some more help too."

Turning, he saw about a dozen men. Some of them had tool bags, others had just hammers. All of them looked ready to work. Logan turned back to Bradley. "You don't have to do this. We'll get it. Eventually, but we'll get it."

Bradley nodded. "I know that, but this is payback for something." He looked at Lizzy and winked. "Your mate did me a favor and I owe her. This is my way of thanking you both."

Logan and Lizzy were putting the lamps together at the now cleared off kitchen table when he asked her what she'd done. She flushed, and he thought this was going to be good.

"His daughter was parking."

Logan took a few seconds to realize what she was saying.

"And when I caught them together, I…well, I made them see the errors of their ways."

Logan laughed. "And just how did you do that? Don't tell me that you made the boy go limp in front of his girl? Oh, Lizzy, he'll never live that down."

"No, I made them see…" She cleared her throat. "They both know what it feels like to have a baby. *All* the pain of having a child."

"You didn't."

She nodded.

"How much did you make them hurt? I'm betting if Bradley is this happy, you did a great job."

"I made an impression. I think the boy was more afraid than she was. Men don't like to think about a baby coming out of them right there."

Logan laughed. He was in tears by the time Bradley walked in to see what was so funny. By the time the lamps were finished, the two of them were still laughing so hard he thought he would be sore for a month. Finally, regaining some control, Logan looked at his new friend when he asked him about the trial.

"It went well. I think something happened afterwards, though. I sort of got this rush of magic or something when I picked up the book of spells I was looking for. Lizzy got it too."

"You did. Both of you did. Do you know what it smells like to me?"

Logan shivered, not liking the smile on Bradley's face.

"You might be glad you're sitting down."

Logan closed his eyes. This was not going to be good. Not good at all. He opened his eyes again and shook his head. Nope, he decided, he really didn't want to know. When Bradley got up and walked away, Logan sat there for several minutes before he stood up to find out.

"Fuck." He ran down the hall toward the kitchen. "Hey, Bradley. Wait up."

About the Author

Kathi Barton, author of the bestselling series Force of Nature, lives in Nashport, Ohio with her husband Paul. In addition to writing full time Kathi likes to spend time with her eight grandkids, three children and three children-in-laws. She writes to relax and have fun.

Her muse, a cross between Jimmy Stewart and Hugh Jackman brings them to life for her readers in a way that has them coming back time and again for more. Her favorite genre is paranormal romance with a great deal of spice. You can visit Kathi on line and drop her an email if you'd like. She loves hearing from her fans. aaronskiss@gmail.com.

Follow Kathi on her blog:
http://kathisbartonauthor.blogspot.com/

www.ingramcontent.com/pod-product-compliance
Lightning Source LLC
Chambersburg PA
CBHW020620180626
46810CB00007B/2864